better off famous?

Also by Jane Mendle

Kissing in Technicolor

A NOVEL

better off famous?

Jane Mendle

 ST. MARTIN'S GRIFFIN ⚹ NEW YORK

This is a work of fiction. All of the characters, organizations, and events portrayed in this novel are either products of the author's imagination or are used fictitiously.

www.stmartins.com

Library of Congress Cataloging-in-Publication Data

Mendle, Jane.
    Better off famous? / Jane Mendle.—1st ed.
        p. cm.
    Summary: Tired of being average, sixteen-year-old Annie auditions for a television show while visiting her great aunt in New York City and soon finds her life turned upside-down, as the amazing benefits of fame are overcome by temptations and the ever-present paparazzi.
    ISBN-13: 978-0-312-36903-3
    ISBN-10: 0-312-36903-4
    1. Celebrities—Fiction. 2. Actors and actresses—Fiction. 3. Conduct of life Fiction. 4. Aunts—Fiction. 5. Paparazzi—Fiction. 6. New York (N. Y.)—Fiction. I. Title.

PZ7 .M52538Bet   2007
[Fic]—dc22
                                            2007023913

First Edition: November 2007

10 9 8 7 6 5 4 3 2 1

better off famous?

prologue

So forgive me: I was tired of my life. Yes, I know there are starving, bald-headed children who need only the price of a cup of coffee per day for their permanent rescue and nourishment. Well, I never pretended to be Mother Teresa. I never even pretended to be the girl next door. It just kind of happened that I ended up as America's tabloid darling—all dimples and pink sweaters and artificially glossy hair. Frankly, I bore as much resemblance to that totally phony image of myself as I did to a UNICEF ad.

Which is why, I suppose, I self-detonated and turned into a teenage Cruella DeVil and ended up drunk and glaring from the very same supermarket tabloids that once splashed up my peachy-sweet photos. "Gone Wild," screamed the headlines. Greasy, teary mascara crusted the lids of my unfocused eyes. Something that was either champagne or drool glistened across the top of my very expensive, very tiny turquoise top. A picture supposedly speaks a thousand words, but at least these photos didn't actually replicate the stream of half-lucid four-letter words I'd spewed at the paparazzi.

The craziest thing about it all? I was never that different from who the magazines thought I was. I was like you. I was like everyone. I was a totally boring goody-goody from a small Alabama town. I was never the most popular or the most unpopular kid. Truthfully, I was kind of average until my life went from snooze to snazztastic in about sixty seconds. I didn't mind being that airbrushed plastic Annie Hoffman doll as much as I should have. In fact, I kind of loved it.

(Insert appropriate blush here.)

Everyone, it seems, is interested in the rise and fall of Annie Hoffman. Preachers, comedians, psychologists . . . they talk about me like I'm some kind of phenomenon, a teenage Hester Prynne with a denim-clad cult following the size of New Delhi. It amazes me that so many very important people know my name. Like doesn't the president need to do something involving running the country rather than talking about how I (yes, me!) represent the tragedy of American youth? You'd think gang violence was more or less nonexistent.

Everyone wants to know how this thing, this horrifying transformation, happened. But the whole shebang was a good deal less scandalous than the media would have you believe. It started, simply enough, with a small phobia and a bad day.

chapter 1

The sweat began, as always, in my palms. It was 11:00 A.M. on Friday, June 13, and my drippy hands had now existed, *ex utero,* for precisely sixteen years and five hours. I wiped my palms on my tank top and smiled weakly at the driving evaluator.

Honestly? I wanted a driver's license about as much as I wanted to join an ashram in Tibet and be forced to greet the dawn every morning in a state of spiritual enlightenment. That is to say, not at all. It's not that I didn't understand the need to drive. I had waited for enough rides and walked home from enough bus stops to understand the allure of climate-controlled motion. And I certainly didn't mind being in a car with someone else driving. It's really what happened when *I* held the steering wheel that was a problem. At this exact moment, I could feel the points of my fingers burning against the wheel, an epicenter for all the queasiness and sweat flooding my body.

Deep breaths were proving radically unhelpful.

The examiner's squeaky voice interrupted my daymare.

"Reverse," she said. She had on a "Doris" name tag and the sort of tight gray curls that involve sleeping on a scalpful of foam curlers. She looked like the kind of person who would complain, after winning a day at a spa, about the quality of her seaweed wrap. With another nervous smile, I slipped the Honda from Park to R and lightly touched the gas pedal.

The car whirled out of the parking space. Reflexively, I smashed on the brakes, and the Honda bounced into position.

Doris, who presumably had endured plenty of rough reversals in her career, bobbed her sausage curls and made a conspicuous mark on her pad.

"You're facing the wrong way," she said, oozing displeasure.

"Huh?" I responded articulately.

"This is a one-way aisle. You're going the wrong way."

My newly dry palms began to moisten themselves again. I reparked, carefully, and reversed again.

More teenagers die in car accidents than by anything else every year, including alcohol poisoning or general humiliation. I don't understand why we continue to insist that it is socially advantageous for people with undeveloped frontal lobes and overeager physical reflexes to be in control of what is basically a metallic, earthbound Death Star.

Doris continued to make small marks on her pad as she directed me down to the main road. I'd driven on Skyland Boulevard before and been just fine, but suddenly, at this precise moment, it looked like the Autobahn. Biting my lip, I turned into the appropriate, far-right lane. I wondered how Doris would react if I put on the radio to help me relax. Gas pedal. Rearview check. Breathe. Count pounding heartbeats. More gas. This was OK. Really. Like Gloria Gaynor, I would survive.

"You missed the turn," Doris said loudly.

I pushed down on the brake pedal. "What?"

"Don't brake!" Doris ordered. The car behind us honked loudly and swerved.

My foot reached for the gas pedal again. I could feel a tremendous nauseous wave curdling over me.

To my knowledge, I was the only person at my high school who did not anticipate my sixteenth birthday with excessive glee. This single fact suggested that it was entirely possible that I had some kind of irrevocable birth defect. Probably, the adventure portion of my genetic code had mutated into dorkiness during the months my mother spent reading Jane Austen during her pregnancy.

"Didn't you hear me telling you to turn?" Doris's curls were wagging in indignation. I concentrated on not puking all over the windshield. Aside from being humiliating, that would dangerously impair visibility.

"No," I whispered.

"I said it four times."

"Oh."

My foot was still tapping the gas pedal in great, shivery jumps.

"Maybe I should pull over," I said, glancing at Doris.

Signaling like a far more in-control driver, I moved onto the shoulder of the road and sat there for a second, the sweat streaming down my neck, willing the nausea to subside. It didn't.

"Excuse me," I said to Doris, and opened the door. Leaning as far away from the Honda as possible, I started retching and heaving. The sickness seemed to last forever. When it was over, I leaned back against the car seat.

The word *mortified* comes from the Latin, *mors, mortis*—meaning "death." Never had I been more mortified, in the actual deadly sense of the word. It would have been marginally preferable had I truly croaked during my driving test, which would at least have spared me explaining the current catastrophe.

"Maybe I should forget about taking the test," I whispered.

"Honey," Doris said tartly, "you've already failed."

chapter 2

Failed.

Failed.

The only other person I know who failed the driving exam was Martin Horner. He failed it four times and his parents had already bought him a bright blue Volkswagen Beetle, which sat in the driveway for three months until he finally managed to get his license. The day he passed the test, he drove around the high school parking lot screaming, "Horny M rocks," at the top of his lungs.

Martin Horner is psycho. According to Tina Reban—whose mother works with Martin's mother, which therefore makes Tina a reputable source—he wasn't on an Outward Bound trip last summer, like he told everyone, but at some camp for disturbed teens.

I wasn't psycho (I didn't think), just star hexed. I take my horoscope pretty seriously, and Mercury was most assuredly in retrograde. Which meant, sweet sixteen or not, I ought to have delayed this whole driving test thing to a more astrologically advisable time.

Doris drove us back to the DMV while I flopped, eviscerated, in the passenger seat. When we got back, my mom was waiting on a bench outside, looking anxious. She jumped up as Doris parked the Honda perfectly straight and equidistant between the yellow lines.

"Annie?"

Doris gazed at her with barely disguised contempt and paused, midwaddle.

"She might need a bit of a stomach stabilizer," she said.
"Annie?"

I could feel tears hovering in my eyes.

"Like I'm the first person ever to throw up during a driving test," I mumbled.

Mom's eyebrows raised automatically. Then she rearranged her face into a completely nonreactive mask. "Maybe you're sick," she said blandly.

"I'm fine."

"I think we should get you home."

No argument there.

"I take it you don't need to do anything else here."

Like get my picture taken? "Uh, no," I mumbled. My lips, it seemed were incapable of fully opening. They were welded in permanent mutter-speak.

Mom patted my shoulder. I wished she wouldn't be so sympathetic. It was making me want to throw things. Or cry. Or throw up again.

Mom dropped me at home and went to work after I assured her—about five times—that I was fine and not about to hurl myself off the roof of the University Club. Both of my parents make worrying their primary hobby, which meant Mom obviously couldn't desert her phobic daughter during the process of semi-permanent emotional scarring. The first thing I did once I was finally alone was crawl into my pajamas, turn the AC down to arctic temperatures, and wallow in my own angst and misery. I'd been diligently wallowing for about twenty minutes when the door flew open.

"Annie!" squealed my little brother Nathan. He's eleven. And loud. I pulled the pillow over my head.

"What are you doing?"

"Wallowing," I mumbled into the pillow. "It requires solitude."

"What?"

"I'm wallowing," I repeated. Someday, science will discover a method for instantaneously dissolving small boys. At present, I had to rely on more primitive methodology.

"Go away."

"Can I see your license?"

"*Get out!*" I screamed, heaving my pillow at the door.

"Yo yo yo," he said, ducking and tossing a handful of envelopes at the bed. "I just brought you your mail."

I retrieved the envelopes from where they'd fallen. "Feel free to shut the door behind you."

Nathan closed the door and stood expectantly inside my room. I giggled, despite myself.

"I meant *leave* the room and then shut the door behind you," I specified. "Wallowing is a private endeavor."

Nathan shrugged but didn't move. I threw myself back down on the bed and began opening my mail.

The first envelope was from my friend Sarah. She sends me a birthday card every year, even though she lives ten minutes away and I see her pretty much every day. Sarah is so overwhelmingly, genuinely nice that it's unbelievable. Like I'd be shocked if the same disgruntled teenage thoughts that seem to be a permanent part of my gray matter repertory have ever entered her skull.

The second envelope turned out to be from this music camp I'm going to in July, with a list of all the stuff I should bring. They actually specified *violin* on the list.

The third envelope was the major one, the one that—though I didn't yet know it—was going to change my boring life irrevocably and miraculously. It was from my great-aunt Alexandra. In theory, a card from Aunt Alexandra should have been unusual but not particularly important. I've only met her twice, once when I was so small I couldn't remember it and once when I was eleven and we went to New York. She didn't even come to my Bat Mitzvah, but she did send a card with the second biggest check I got. (The biggest was from my mom's brother, who lives in California and invented some brilliant one-inch piece of metal that's good for computers. We haven't visited him in California even though I keep telling my parents that it would be a valuable cultural experience. Uncle Tim *did* come to the Bat Mitzvah, with this amazingly tall woman who wore leather pants and had never heard of the Torah, supposedly because she was raised a Mormon. She was a pretty valuable cultural eye-opener all by herself.)

At any rate, the card from Aunt Alexandra wasn't even a birthday card. It was really thick cream-colored paper with edges that were meant to look torn and said *Mrs. Alexandra Hoffman Schlesinger* in curly script on the front.

Inside it said:

> *Annie, dear—*
>
> *I understand your sixteenth birthday is at hand. I thought perhaps a trip to New York would be a good way to celebrate.*
>
> *With affection,*
> *Your Aunt Alexandra*

There was a folded piece of paper. I unfolded it. It was an itinerary from a travel agency on Madison Avenue, listing a round-trip ticket from Birmingham, Alabama, to LaGuardia in New York, in the name of Annie Hoffman.

I started screaming.

Seriously.

It was like I was that guy gymnast who fell off the vault and then managed to get the gold medal at the Olympics anyway. (Even though I'm not sure that was particularly fair, given the presumable standards of international competition and all that.)

Until I started screaming, I had forgotten that Nathan was still in my room, welded like a barnacle to my wicker rocker.

"Chill out, Sistah," Nathan drawled. (Why he attempts to sound like a 1980s Spike Lee extra is beyond me. I guess we don't fully understand all the possible genetic manifestations of dweebdom yet.)

"I'm going to New York," I explained. I handed him Aunt Alexandra's letter.

"Rockin'."

I rolled over and picked up the phone to call my dad.

"Failed?" Dad answered the phone.

"What?" I was confused for a minute, until I remembered the revolting motor vehicle humiliation I'd suffered at my own incompetent hands. "Never mind," I said, "I've been invited to New York." I could hear his mind whirling as I explained Aunt Alexandra's letter to him. "So can I go?"

"But that's the first week of your music camp," he said immediately.

Sigh. I love playing the violin. It's just about the only thing that turns off my overactive brain. But this was *New York.* How could I turn down New York to spend a week in North Carolina with a bunch of social outcast musicians?

"Camp's an entire month," I whined. "So I'll take a week off."

"But you really wanted to go to music camp. You were begging us to let you go."

"Dad! Let me repeat myself: This is *New York.*"

Perhaps the reason I'm a deformed freak with unfortunate reaction times is because my parents are clones of each other. So instead of getting some good, Darwinian, survival-of-the-fittest genetic adaptations, I inherited the exact same bizarre, clone DNA on both sides.

When I told Mom about the letter, she said, "But you really wanted to go to music camp."

Arrrggggghhh!

But they agreed to call the camp and tell them I'd be there a week late.

"You're so lucky," said my friend Sarah later that night.

"I can't believe you *failed*," said my friend Meg.

We had gone to the Crimson Café to celebrate my birthday. This is because the guy behind the counter is indescribably divine and almost, *almost* recognizes me when I come in, which is often. Also, it is right by the university and Meg wants to be hit on by a college student, preferably an artsy, sophisticated one who wears a beret and talks about obscure German philosophers. Not that Meg has read any philosophy. Plus, the one time that a college student actually did hit on us, he was completely stumbling drunk and kept petting Meg's hair until she freaked and hid in the bathroom until the guy left and Sarah and I retrieved her.

"You cannot, I repeat, *cannot* tell anyone that I failed," I emphasized.

Sarah giggled. "You can retake the test in two weeks."

I shook my head. "I'm going to be in New York in two weeks. And then I go straight to camp. Like, literally. My parents are picking me up at the airport and driving me straight there."

"Well, good, then you'll still want this." Sarah reached down into her red bag and deposited a silver-wrapped package in front of me. "It's from both of us," she added.

"Ooh!" I began shredding the paper. "Hey!" I exclaimed, looking down at the cheerful sarong and beach towel.

"See, we figured you had to have some time to lounge around that fancy pool that's in the brochure."

"And we know how much you hate wearing a bikini," Meg added.

Well, yes. Personally, I believe the current bathing suit culture breeds insecurity and objectifies women and is a slap in the face to the suffragettes who went on hunger strikes for women's rights. But really? I just hate feeling *that naked* in public.

"This is awesome." I grinned. "I'll definitely use this."

"Good." Meg pulled out a pack of Camels and lit one.

I absolutely hate it when Meg smokes.

"What are you doing?" I hissed. "We're in public."

Meg waved the smoke away. Meg would not be particularly Goth if we lived someplace remotely cool like the East Village. Because we live in Alabama, she is about as Goth as it gets. Her black-tipped nails made the smoke waving pretty dramatic.

"It's just a cigarette," she said. "Jeez, Annie, you need to chill out." She inhaled and tried to blow a smoke ring, but it ended up being more of a smoke C.

"Meg," I hissed again. She stubbed out the cigarette and gave me an exasperated look. I didn't care.

"You're so lucky," Sarah said again, probably to change the subject. "What's your Aunt Alexandra like?"

I paused. "Actually," I realized, "I don't really know."

chapter 3

This may sound kind of dopey, but it wasn't until I got on the airplane that I realized I'd never flown by myself before. I mean, I knew the routine—seat belt, peanuts, trashy mystery—but there was this freaky moment when I felt like I might not be able to pull it off. I have a long history of botching truly wonderful opportunities. Like, if my life were *Arabian Nights,* I'd somehow manage to fall off the magic carpet.

Here's what I learned: Flying by yourself is just as boring as flying with your parents. No one notices or comments on you. The businessmen with their laptops stay absorbed in their work; the screaming babies scream; the "stay in your seat" sign is always lit whenever you have to go the bathroom. But the instant I got off the plane in New York, I felt suddenly a lot older and even possibly a bit cooler. Mom and Dad had made sure I had Aunt Alexandra's address and money for a taxi, so I ended up wheeling my suitcase in the direction of the "Baggage Claim, Street, Taxis" sign like I'd been jet-setting since birth.

Outside, cars were orbiting the airport at warp speed. I was walking toward a yellow cab when this woman shoved past me and knocked my suitcase over. The zipper, which was missing a couple of teeth, popped open and my clothes began leaking onto the pavement.

"Get in line, kid," the woman snarled.

"Yeah, there's a line," another voice chimed in. When I turned around, I noticed a big sign reading "Taxi Stand" and the longest line of people standing behind it. I mean, I've been to Alabama football games and Six Flags and there is only one Coke machine in my entire high school, but this line dwarfed anything I had ever seen before. In minor shock, I scraped my clothes back into the suitcase and dutifully joined the end of the queue.

When it was finally my turn for a taxi, I explained to the driver that he should be careful with my suitcase, so that it didn't pop open again.

"Yeah, got it," he answered, hurling it in the trunk with a re-sounding thud. I crossed my fingers that the bag stayed shut. There is only so much public underwear viewing I can manage in a day. As we flew over the Triboro Bridge, the theme music from *Working Girl* (which is one of my favorite movies) began running through my head.

At long last, my exceptionally mundane life had a sound track.

I knew I'd met Aunt Alexandra before, but I didn't remember her. It turned out that she was hardly the plump and Disneyfied fairy godmother I'd been expecting. According to my anatomy teacher last year, the frontal lobe is responsible for impulsive be-havior. In that case, I think Aunt Alexandra has a frontal lobe the size of a gnat. I realize that she and I are not exactly close re-lations, but it's difficult to believe that we share even the small-est snip of DNA.

When she opened the door, she announced, "Ah, Annie! Come in." Then she turned and walked away.

I very hesitantly followed her into a room which looked like what I always assumed a boudoir would look like. There was an actual chaise, which Aunt Alexandra—despite being about sev-enty and possibly arthritic—managed to wilt into as effectively as a Victorian maiden. The chaise was celery colored and there was a matching pale green drink on the table beside it.

"Hi," I said. "Thanks for this trip. It's, um, really spectacular."

"I would offer you a vodka gimlet, but your father appears not to trust you with alcohol," Aunt Alexandra answered. "He was quite firm that I should not offer you anything. Have you had a problem?"

I blinked.

"No, of course not," I said automatically.

Honestly? I haven't come into enough contact with alcohol to have a problem with it. Well, once Meg's parents were out of town and she and I thoroughly plundered the liquor cabinet. (We discovered that Midori tastes like Kool-Aid and Scotch tastes like Listerine, neither of which we had expected.) And there are parties where kids from my school get trashed and smoke pot and stuff, but I never have more than a sip of someone else's warm, nasty beer. Frankly, I'm not such a huge fan of those parties. They're not exactly the monster affairs like you see in movies, with football players smashing lamps and catatonic cheerleaders lining the floor. It's more like an especially out-of-control day in the school parking lot.

I didn't explain this to Aunt Alexandra though. Instead, I just walked closer to the chaise, since it felt strange to talk to someone from all the way across the room.

"Don't feel obligated to kiss the old crone," she announced. She had a rich, bubbling voice that filled the entire room. It was pretty theatrical.

I smiled and leaned forward to kiss her on the cheek anyway.

"We're going to Jacques' tonight."

"Is that a person?"

"A restaurant." Aunt Alexandra sighed. "I do hope you're not so provincial as to unappreciate French food."

Was *unappreciate* a word? I wasn't sure.

"I like French food," I said aloud.

Aunt Alexandra sniffed. She had sort of a beaky face, all

sharp and pointed in the places where it should have been round.

"You," she said accusingly, "have an *accent.*"

"An accent?"

Aunt Alexandra nodded. I noticed she had a small mole on her temple. She probably referred to it as a beauty mark.

"A *southern* accent," she emphasized.

I paused, then said it anyway. "I do not."

OK, I'm from the South. I admit that. But an accent? Come on. No one in my circle of friends has a southern accent, and if I somehow (long shot) had managed to develop one, I would have known about it before now.

Aunt Alexandra apparently disagreed. "Yes, child, I'm afraid you sound quite southern," she said. She gave me one of those prolonged up-and-down stares. I felt myself shriveling.

"What year in school are you?" she continued.

"I'm about to start the eleventh grade."

Aunt Alexandra nodded. "Eleventh," she mused. "Sixteen is such a nice age." Then her nose and brows and cheeks and other pointy features drew together until her face was practically a pyramid. "I have twenty-four years of education, you know," she said.

Well, evidently none of them were spent at charm school.

chapter 4

It turns out that Aunt Alexandra sleeps till ten every day, then has breakfast in bed and reads the *Times* until eleven. Her masseuse arrives at 11:30 and spends an hour pummeling her into relaxation. If I had Aunt Alexandra's life, I wouldn't need assistance relaxing. I would be so relaxed that I would practically be an amoeba.

On my third day in the city, before she woke up, I grabbed my violin case and headed out the door. I wasn't trying, exactly, to sneak around. On the other hand, I didn't want to explain what I was doing either.

I mean, what if she wanted to *come*?

I might have to kill her—my very own über-generous, overly eccentric, sometimes rude great-aunt—just to keep her quiet about the whole affair. It would be pretty Mafia.

So instead I went down to the lobby and asked Jules, the supercute doorman, if he would hail a cab for me to Lincoln Center.

"Lincoln Center? You can walk. It's only ten minutes."

"Really?"

Jules pointed. "Straight till you hit Amsterdam, then make a left and follow it downtown till you reach Sixty-sixth Street. You can't miss it."

Well, I swear I never turned off, but I somehow managed to end up on first Broadway and then Columbus Avenue. Only in New York would a straight line be the longest distance between two points. I'd had butterflies in my stomach ever since I'd woken up that morning. Now, they morphed into something more like velociraptors. This had been a terrible, terrible idea, a world-class demonstration of stupidity.

In desperation, I stuck my hand in the air tentatively. A taxi whisked up beside me. At that moment, it felt like magic. I, Annie Hoffman, had hailed a cab. Honestly, why should I even bother having a driver's license if I possessed such a remarkable ability to raise my arm and have a car appear?

"Lincoln Center, please."

The driver looked at me like I was crazy. "It's right there," he said, pointing.

"Where?"

"There."

All I could see were a lot of buses and people and ten lanes of traffic.

"Where?" I asked, feeling increasingly trapped in an unfortunate "Who's on First?" imitation.

"There." The driver sighed loudly. "That big building there on the corner is the Juilliard School. On the other side of it are Avery Fisher Hall and the Opera House."

"Got it. Thanks!" I hopped back onto the street, feeling a good deal less competent than I had sixty seconds ago. But at least now I knew where I was supposed to go.

Here's one of my deepest, darkest secrets: I'd been snooping around the Juilliard Web site pretty regularly for a couple years now. Juilliard is *the* best music school in the country. It's not like I really thought I was Juilliard caliber on the violin. It was just . . . well, I wanted to go. If I could. Which, OK, maybe I couldn't.

But they have this precollege program and I *know* all of the types of pieces they require for the audition and *they were having open auditions exactly when I happened to be in New York*. As far as I was concerned, that was karma of the most amazing and fateful type.

(If only I weren't so nervous. As far as I know, I have never fainted, but it's a new experience I could live without.)

Inside, it was easy to find the auditions, because there were signs and arrows everywhere. I saw kids with cases for violins, violas, cellos, oboes, clarinets—any instrument you could think of. Some of them looked pretty young. I walked over to the table for last names F–I. My mouth felt like I had just inhaled a pile of sawdust.

"Um, hi, my name is Annie Hoffman," I told the woman. "I wanted to audition for the violin."

I had managed to get the words out. There was no turning back now.

The woman began flipping through a sheaf of paper. "Hoffman, Hoffman," she muttered. She looked up. "I don't see you on the list. When did you register?"

"I didn't," I said softly. "I didn't know you had to."

How could I have missed the part about registration? I had spent hours trolling the Web site. *Courage under fire, Annie . . .*

The woman looked at me. "You do," she said. "I'm sorry."

I could feel tears, inanely, beginning to hover in my eyes.

"Me, too," I whispered. "Thanks anyway."

I turned to leave.

"Wait," the woman said. "We're having another round of auditions in October. I can sign you up for those now."

"That's really nice of you to offer," I said. "But I live too far away."

"Where?"

"Alabama."

The woman nodded. "You have an accent."

I do *not*.

"Did you come up here just for this?" she asked.

"No." I shook my head. "I'm visiting my great-aunt, but I just thought maybe, you know . . ." The tears, unspilled, were now under control. Perhaps there was hope for my future emotional competency.

She looked at me again. Her head tilted. "Do you have an audition program prepared?"

"Yeah. I read what you needed on the Web site and I'm ready to go."

The woman tilted her head even more. "Your name is Hoffman, right? I can fit you in at eleven fifteen."

"*What??* Oh, thank you so much! I'm so incredibly thrilled," I gushed.

She laughed. "Just play well. Good luck."

Now I *really* felt strange.

Thirty minutes of conversation established that the kids in the Juilliard waiting room were abnormal. They were like Stepford children. They were gross, gross androids who didn't have friends who flirted with college students or brothers who snotted out milk mucus when they laughed. They had never heard of *The OC,* thought Heath Ledger was the name of a candy bar, and none of them (not *one*) had read a single Harry Potter book, let alone an issue of *Us.*

If I were stranded alone on a desert island, I would have better conversations with coconuts. Seriously.

I have to say that I looked the best, though. I was wearing this great pink skirt that Aunt Alexandra and I had gotten the day before in Bloomingdale's. All the guys wore blah khakis and blah navy blazers. The girls had droopy, awful olive- and gray-colored clothing, like the orphans in *Annie.* My own personal Dorkiness Quotient began to recede in the face of such truly challenged social proficiency.

I mostly forgot about the audition while I was talking to the other kids. But around eleven I began to feel weird and awful again. It was a good thing that I didn't play the flute or anything where my inability to breathe might affect my music.

"Are you nervous?" the girl next to me asked.

Frankly, I felt like that guy who gave birth in *Alien* must have right before the alien baby came out. But there was no need to advertise that.

"Not at all," I lied as casually as possible.

Then they called my name. Tentatively, I walked into the audition room. It was cold inside and completely empty, except for a long folding table. The judges, *six* of them, were arranged in an intimidating row behind it. In unison, they whipped their pens and clipboards upward. Nervously, I balled up my hands into fists, then released them immediately. I couldn't afford to have any kind of finger cramp now.

"Hi," I mumbled, trying to smile.

"Hoffman," said a round man at the end of the table. He had about three strands of hair on his head and had combed them over as precisely as possible.

"Yeah," I said. "Um, I mean, yes, sir."

"Why don't you begin with your adagio piece?"

I knelt to open my violin case. Closing my eyes, I wrapped my fingers around the bow, pinky and thumb extended. The bow felt just like it always did in my hand. Opening my eyes, I began to breathe again.

chapter 5

So I *rocked* the audition.

If violin playing were like fireworks, my Paganini would be the kind with three colors that explodes into shapes. It was Fourth of July, grand-finale good. I could feel my fingers doing exactly the right thing and I was able to zone out and play rather than be nervous. One of the judges even smiled at me when I was done. Keeping the smile off my face was not a possibility. As soon as I left, I ran and hid in a bathroom stall, where I collapsed with general relief.

This would totally show all those "I've taken violin in New York City since the age of two with this famous guy with a long Russian name that you never heard of" kids in the waiting room.

I got a callback for that afternoon. I thought Aunt Alexandra might be worried about me, so I called to let her know that I was "wandering around and getting to know the city."

She said, sort of dreamily, "Well, just be back in time for dinner. I made a reservation at Isabella's for us."

I had no idea how I would endure my obsessively hovering parents ever again.

When I went back in for the callback, the audition room had gotten even colder. This was probably just in case the judges themselves weren't sufficiently freezing the blood in my veins.

"We'd like you to sight-read," the round man said, gesturing to the music stand in the center of the room. Slowly, I walked over to the stand and studied the piece on it. The page was so thickly covered with musical markings that there was almost no blank space. Personally, I have always held that the optimal black-to-white ratio for a page of music should be roughly equivalent to the black-to-white ratio of a Dalmatian dog. What I was staring at was more like the sheet music equivalent of a purebred Labrador.

"Can I have a minute?" I asked.

"One minute," said the round man precisely. I wouldn't have been surprised if he'd pulled out a timer. As it was, the ticking of the clock seemed very loud.

I stared at the page grimly for another second, then tucked my violin under my chin. When I set the bow down on the strings, I had a bit too much pressure; there was a hoarse echo as I started to play. Unlike the first audition round, where I was pretty much unaware of anything other than the music, it now seemed like all my senses were going at full force: I heard each tentative note boomed out in the vacant room, felt my skin goose-bumped with cold. Even the slight pressure between the bow and my fingers was almost painful. I'd spent the past year dreaming of being at a Juilliard audition and now I would have given just about anything to be back at home in my sweatpants.

After the callback was over, I walked outside and sat on a concrete bench, just watching people go by while I waited for the results to be announced. I didn't really feel like talking to anyone, let alone one of the Stepford musicians.

I'd been there for a pretty long time when one of the judges came out. It was the one who had smiled at me during the first round. She had a thick gray bun, like a ball of yarn.

"You're Hoffman, correct?" she asked.

I nodded.

"Your playing has a very light feel to it," she said.

Was that good? Did she mean light, like bright, or lite, like flimsy?

"Oh," I said. Then, because I couldn't stand it, I asked, "Is that good?"

The judge lit a cigarette and inhaled deeply. Her lungs were about to pop out.

"It's quite nice," she said.

"Thanks."

I began to revise my opinion of the sight-reading. My playing was nice! Quite nice, in fact. She wouldn't say that if she didn't mean it. In fact, can judges even compliment you? *I had to be going to Juilliard.* I mean, I could probably sue for false hope and loss of sanity if I didn't make it in.

I imagined how I would explain this to my parents and friends.

I just thought I would give it a shot. . . .

They would all be squeaking they would be so impressed.

I mean, Juilliard. On the violin.

I began to think about how I would break the news to Aunt Alexandra that I needed to move in with her.

chapter 6

I hadn't thought there could be anything worse in the world than failing the driving test. I was wrong.

Not getting into Juilliard was way, way worse.

I stared at the audition list disbelievingly. It wasn't in alphabetical order, so maybe I'd somehow—like, ha—just missed my name on it. After the third time through, I gave up. I mean, would it kill Mercury to get out of retrograde one of these days? My horoscope was unquestionably ruining my life. Before anyone could see me dissolve, I turned and fled the building.

For a few seconds, I had deluded myself into thinking I could escape the endless ho-humminess of my life. But instead of a semi-glam, cosseted New York existence, I was going to end up back in Bryant High. It was going to be another long year of eating cardboard pizza in the cafeteria and wondering why Kale McLaughlin was dating Cindy Peters instead of me. I'd probably get a top locker, with a combination I wouldn't be able to reach. Instead of taking violin with the stars, I'd be taking trig. There are *jails* with more lenient attendance policies than Mr. Slepak's math class.

Wildly, I tore through Lincoln Center and somehow ended up in a dead-end collection of Dumpsters. I spun around and went the other direction. Tears were falling off my face and down my neck into the collar of my shirt.

There was no exit this way either. Was this just more evidence of why I didn't belong at Juilliard? Maybe real musicians were born knowing their way around this place, sort of like a geographical perfect pitch. Then I ran into someone. I mean, literally. My blubbery face went smack against his nice French blue shirt and left a wet mark.

"Whoa, watch it," he said.

"Sorry," I muttered. My voice was thick from the crying, so it came out as "thorry." Then, I added, "How do you get out of here, anyway?"

"Where do you need to go?"

Why should that matter? Was he planning to follow me?

"The street," I said. "Any street. I need to get out of here."

He took my elbow and began guiding me. "You're crying, aren't you?" he observed.

A master detective . . .

"No comment," I answered. I looked at the guy. He was pretty old, with spiky silver hair and wire-rim glasses. I didn't like that he was holding my elbow.

"Is everything OK?" he asked.

"Well, if it were," I said, "do you think I would be running in circles and howling like a wildebeest?" I pulled my elbow away from him and wiped my face with my hand. Then I felt bad.

"I'm sorry," I said formally. "That was totally rude of me. Damsels in distress aren't supposed to snap at their chivalrous rescuers." I set down the violin case and dried my teary hand on my skirt. At this point, I was probably 98 percent saline.

"Do you play the violin?" the man asked. He made a sharp right between two buildings. I picked up the violin case and trotted along behind him.

"Not well enough to get into Juilliard," I said. As soon as the words escaped, I could feel the tears surging up again. I smashed my lips together in an effort to contain them.

The guy was quiet. Then he said, "It's pretty hard to get into Juilliard."

"I got a callback," I said softly. Then I added, truthfully, "It's kind of funny. You're the only one who really knows I came to the audition. I didn't want to tell my family or friends."

"Why not?"

We turned again. "In case I didn't get in," I admitted, laughing a little. "I don't know that anyone takes my violin playing really seriously. Me included." I wiped my still-sticky eyes with my free hand.

The guy reached into his coat pocket and handed me a handkerchief. It was pale gray and silky. It looked much too nice to use mopping myself up.

"You must be pretty good even to have gotten a callback," he said.

"Maybe." I paused for a minute and twisted the hanky around my fingers. "See, the problem is that I'm good at lots of things. Like, I'm good at violin and at swimming and at schoolwork and stuff. But I'm not *really* good at anything and I wish I were." I shrugged. "I get tired of being average all the time."

"Hmm," the guy said.

He turned again. I had no idea where we were now.

That's when I began to have a really awful queasy feeling. I was following a strange (spiky-haired!) man around New York City, spilling my most intimate secrets to him. I was probably going to end up dead and in a Dumpster before morning.

"Where are you taking me?" I demanded.

"Sixty-third Street."

"Are you sure?"

"Yes." He stopped and stared at me. My creepy vibe accelerated. "Unless you have time to come with me for a moment," he added.

I began backing away. "Oh no, definitely not."

He laughed. "Relax. I'm a producer. We're holding auditions today at the dramatic academy for a new teenage TV show. There's a part for a violinist."

"A likely story," I said, still backing away.

"No, here." He began reaching in his coat again.

I watched his hand root around under his coat and waited for him to pull out a gun or a rag drenched in chloroform or something. (Did chloroform still exist?) It would not be an exaggeration to say that my life flashed before my eyes in slow motion. I wished that I had told *someone* I was coming to Juilliard today. Sarah, certainly, wouldn't have laughed at me.

The man pulled out a harmless white business card and handed it to me. Automatically, I took it.

Gilbert Grayle
Grayle-Kaufman-Bond Productions

My heart was still thudding violently. "This doesn't prove anything," I said. "Anyone can get cards printed."

He nodded. "Sure," he agreed. "But I really am a TV producer." He looked at me very closely. The scrutiny made me feel uncomfortable. "What's your name, sweetheart?"

"Annie," I whispered, still backing away from him. *I told him my name.* What was wrong with me? I was so ending up in a Dumpster.

"Annie, it's OK. My number is on that card. I really am a producer. We're looking for kids to star in a new teen drama called *Country Day.* I think you resemble a character in the script named Berry and I'd like you to audition for her, even if you haven't done any acting." He gave me the unsettling, scrutinizing look again. "We'll be casting until Monday. Think about it, talk it over with your parents, and give me a call if you like."

That sounded a little more authentic, but I still didn't trust him.

"Where's Sixty-third Street?" I asked. We were still deep in the maze of Lincoln Center. All I could see were large concrete buildings.

Gilbert Grayle pointed to a building on the corner. "Turn right at that corner and you'll be out," he said.

I grabbed my violin case and practically ran away from him. When I was at the corner, I turned around. He was still looking at me.

"Thanks," I said.

chapter 7

Aunt Alexandra may have had a very small Picasso and a sapphire ring the size of my head, but she did not have e-mail. After dinner, she went back to the apartment while I found an Internet café and messaged Meg that I had been offered a TV audition today.

Her reply: *Are you sure it's not for the Playboy network?*

Oh, ha ha. Now that's a knee-slapper. Even though I hadn't told Meg about the Juilliard fiasco, IMing her made me feel a lot better about things.

After we were done, I walked the three blocks back to Aunt Alexandra's apartment. Even after my morning's adventure, being alone in New York was strange. I felt somehow conspicuous—like I had forgotten to wear some crucial article of clothing, or was walking around with something gross on my face, or had been spotted at the Crimson Café on a day I had stayed home sick. (All of which have happened to me before.)

Jules, the doorman, greeted me cheerfully. He, at least, seemed to think I belonged in the city.

"Little Miss H.! How was dinner?"

Jules is the only person on the planet I can imagine allowing to call me Little Miss. He looks like a sculpture. He's very, very dark, with three-dimensional cheekbones and biceps that bulge like footballs under his uniform. I am developing an absolutely mountainous crush on him.

"Good," I answered, leaning against the door and looking up at him. Jules is almost an entire foot taller than I am. "So you know my great-aunt better than I do. Do you think she would take me to get my eyebrow pierced?"

I fingered the right brow tentatively as I spoke. I am a big baby when it comes to pain. But I've wanted my eyebrow pierced for almost as long as I've wanted to go to Juilliard. I had a vague feeling that my parents would grow fangs and snap off my head, Pez dispenser fashion, if I appeared with a pierced eyebrow. On the other hand, if someone with obvious taste and style like Aunt Alexandra had allowed me to get it, they might be more reasonable. (I hoped.)

"Baby girl, why you want to do that? Such a pretty face! The good Lord gave you two holes in your nose and one in your mouth and you don't need any more than that."

I giggled. My crush on Jules was reaching Alpine proportions.

"Juuuules," I said, doing something (involuntarily) that was best described as batting my eyelashes. "Do you think Aunt Alexandra would even notice if I got my eyebrow pierced?" I added.

Jules made a sort of disgusted throaty groan. "Such a pretty face and Annie H. wants to put a hole in it. She'll look like a Christmas tree." This latter comment was not directed at me but at a man who was entering the building. The man stopped his brisk, city-slicker speed walk and looked directly at me.

Gilbert Grayle.

I shrieked. Jules and Gilbert both winced.

"He's following me!" I blurted, moving closer to Jules.

Jules laughed. "Oooh, Little Miss, you're a funny girl."

"No, Jules, really. He led me all through this really scary part of Lincoln Center and fed me these lies about being a TV producer so I would follow him, probably into a torture chamber out of *Silence of the Lambs,* and now he's here!" I turned and buried my face in Jules's uniform so I didn't have to look at the stalker. It was surprisingly pleasant to be nestled so close to Jules. But after a second, he put a hand on my neck and directed my head upward. He was smiling. Gilbert Grayle was also smiling. I wasn't sure why, unless (heaven forbid) I was on *Candid Camera* and the *entire world* was going to know about the disaster of my life.

"Miss H. This is Mr. Grayle. He lives in Apartment Seventeen-C. And he works in television," Jules explained.

"Oh," I said stupidly.

Gilbert Grayle smiled. "Of all the gin joints in the world, she had to walk into mine," he said.

It took me a second to realize he was quoting *Casablanca*. How witty. Now I would definitely follow him down a deserted alley.

Aloud, I said, "You're really a TV producer?"

"Wait here," he said, walking across the lobby into the waiting elevator. The doors closed.

He returned a few minutes later with a shiny red binder. I used the intervening time to explain to Jules exactly how upsetting my afternoon had been. (Jules's sole comment was "hmmph." He can be a man of few words.)

Mr. Grayle sat down on the couch in the lobby and motioned for me to join him. I did, making sure Jules was still within eyeshot. Forget the Alps. My crush was definitely Himalayan, fast approaching Everest-size.

Mr. Grayle opened the binder carefully and handed me a sheet of paper. I read:

Poised to become this fall's hottest series, *Country Day* will shock and entrance you. Beautiful, bratty, and *very* rich, the students at New York Country Day School have the most glamorous city in the world as their playground. But they still worry about life and love and parents and grades—and, most of all, each other. Because sometimes high school can be more than you bargained for, even when it seems like you have it all.

I would *never* watch this show. I would rather take remedial driving every night of the week.

"You want me to be in this?" I asked, still half-expecting *Candid Camera* to appear. "I'm not an actress. Seriously, the only acting I ever do is my Eliza Doolittle impression."

Mr. Grayle (Gilbert? Were we on a first-name basis?) looked questioningly at me.

"In 'Artford, 'Ereford, and 'Ampshire, 'urricanes 'ardly hever 'appen," I dutifully parroted in my best Cockney.

He shuddered. I giggled as he said, "That would not be required for the part of Berry." He handed me another sheet of paper.

Freshman BERRY CALVIN is the new kid on the block. A serious student and talented violin player, Berry's just moved to New York from Atlanta, Georgia. Naïve, stubborn, and wryly witty, Berry feels like she'll never fit in at school. But when she overhears junior popularity queen KIT WINTERS blackmailed into dating senior SNIDER GREEN, Berry can't afford to fade into the Country Day background any longer (episode 3). She takes on Snider and his infamous hard-playing brat pack, and finds herself the new darling of Country Day's most glittering circle.

Below this was a list:

Berry is . . .
Bookish
Sometimes shy
Sometimes awkward
Sometimes prickly
Pretty, but not glamorous
Innocent
Intelligent

Funny—she often uses humor as a defense

Nervy

Independent—she doesn't change who she is or what she believes
    for other people

Honest

A good kid

If obsessive list making was all it took to create television's hottest show, I could probably have a budding career.

"Why's it called *Country Day* if it's set in New York?" I asked.

"Country day schools are ritzy prep schools," Gilbert said. "We wanted to convey an elite atmosphere."

I nodded. "And you, uh, want me to be Berry?" I asked.

Mr. Grayle raised one eyebrow. I love it when people do that. "Darling, you *are* Berry," he said. "All you have to do is show up at the network and prove it."

"And all this time, I thought I was glamorous but not pretty," I said.

Mr. Grayle tapped the description of "funny—she often uses humor as a defense" pointedly.

"I'm sixteen, not fourteen," I countered.

"You look like you could be fourteen, though."

Well, thanks for the ego boost.

"OK," I sighed. Then I grinned. There were worse things than being asked to audition for a TV show. "Take me to your leader."

chapter 8

Friday morning, I lived up to my newfound reputation of nerviness by disturbing Aunt Alexandra's beauty rest. There was no way I was walking into a roomful of TV executives *by myself* to prove how much I naturally resembled a fourteen-year-old named after fruit. My confidence really only extended to singing "I Have Confidence" in the shower.

(It was a good thing *Country Day* wasn't a musical. I'd probably pass out from delirium in front of all the casting people.)

At any rate, after attempting to wake up Aunt Alexandra, I had considerable sympathy for physical therapists who work with people in comas. I mean, honestly. Anyone would have thought she had spent the previous afternoon doing something considerably more fatiguing than helping me memorize lines while nibbling cheesecake at Cafe Lalo. I had, of course, sworn her to secrecy on the whole Berry Calvin affair until after it was over. Despite Gilbert Grayle's optimism, I was less than convinced I had a future in television.

Auditioning for television was nothing like auditioning for Juilliard. We had to get a special pass even to set foot inside the Spider Broadcasting Network building. The pass was bright red and said "Casting" on it. There was a long chain so that I could hang it around my neck. *Très* chic.

I'd been asked to get to the network by no later than 9:30. This was apparently so that hair and makeup could spend an hour and a half redoing what I'd attempted earlier that morning.

Max, my stylist, said I had classic bones underneath "all those" freckles.

"Thanks," I said, as he rubbed something slimy on my face.

"Do you want your monobrow waxed?"

Excuse me?

"I have a monobrow?" I asked with horror.

"*Darling*," Max said pityingly.

I looked around for Aunt Alexandra, who appeared to be showing her favorite Chanel lipstick (Shanghai Red) to a makeup artist across the room.

"Um," I answered indecisively, staring at my face. As far as I could tell, there was no visible line of fur between my brows.

"I mean, if you don't, that's cool," Max continued, tapping one of my hair curlers with a practiced finger. "I understand you're supposed to be the Plain Jane of the show."

"Max," I said, "this is all very damaging to my self-esteem. You don't want me to feel ugly and inferior during my audition."

He put a hot washcloth over my face. "Aren't you a shoo-in? I was told you had the part wrapped up."

I stared at the yellow terry cloth covering my eyes.

"Mind you, you're the fourth or fifth one to come out for this role. I think these guys don't even know what they're looking for." He whipped off the washcloth and began attacking me with a skin-colored paste. "But I have a good feeling about you."

"Why?"

Max continued to spackle my face. "All of the others were tall and blond and had been doing TV since they were babies and were jaded jaded jaded." He paused, sponge in hand. "And you're not."

"No," I agreed.

"So close that mouth and close those eyes and let me make you beautiful."

I didn't argue.

Aunt Alexandra wasn't allowed in the audition room with me. She stayed talking with the other stylists as I followed Max down the hall to a room labeled "Private." He knocked on the door.

"Yes?"

"I have Annie Hoffman for you."

"Yes," the voice said again. Max swung the door open. I stood there, frozen, on the threshold until he gave me a little push inside the room.

"Hi," I said. "I'm Annie." Then, without thinking, I crossed the room to where Gilbert Grayle and three other people sat. And I shook each of their hands.

Three sets of eyebrows raised. Was I not supposed to shake hands? As Mr. Grayle showed me where I was to sit, I heard one of the women mutter, "Enchanting. Grayle, where did you find this child?"

I didn't realize shaking hands was the sort of earnest, goody-two-shoe behavior reserved for naïve fourteen-year-olds. I just thought it was polite. Awkwardly, I started picking a cuticle, then stopped.

"We're just waiting for Crane," Mr. Grayle said.

"Crane?"

"Crane Renfrew. He's playing Jody Holt."

According to the description I'd read, Jody Holt was one of the superpopular kids at Country Day and Berry's next-door neighbor. The scene I'd been asked to prepare was one where Berry confided to Jody how much she hated New York, but I hadn't realized that the real Jody Holt would be coming to my audition.

"Sure," I agreed. There was a row of cameras across the room and I noticed two guys tweaking various knobs and microphones. Then the door opened and Chad Michael Murray sailed in.

Well, OK, it wasn't really Chad, just a look-alike. Floppy golden hair, sculpted face, piercing hazel eyes, incredibly muscular body not hidden by the T-shirt and jeans he wore, and . . .

I was finding it surprisingly difficult to breathe.

"Crane," Gilbert said warmly. "Glad you could make it." He clapped Crane on the shoulder in a sort of good-ole-boy way. "Come meet Annie Hoffman."

"Heeey," Crane said.

And then, like the world's most untrainable monkey, I failed to learn from experience. I grabbed his hand and shook it.

He laughed.

At me.

"Sorry," I muttered, blushing.

He smiled again. When his lips moved, I became surprisingly, acutely, aware of my own mouth.

"Don't be nervous," Crane said. He sat in the chair opposite me. "I know they said you're not an actor. So just act totally natural, like you did just now, and you'll be cool."

"Uh-huh," I mumbled. I could feel the blush spreading from my cheeks into my scalp and through my ears.

"I mean it," Crane repeated.

"I'm not nervous." As soon as the words were out of my mouth, I realized that it was mostly true. I wasn't an actor and this wasn't like Juilliard, where I had invested a lot of time and hope and energy into that particular goal. I just had to get through this whole thing without acting stupid. Crane looked as though he didn't believe me, so I smiled my best imitation of a nervy Berry Calvin smile.

"I'm a natural," I joked, striking an elegant Norma Desmond pose. Crane laughed again, a breezy, natural laugh. I felt the blush receding.

Gilbert Grayle had been conferring with the camera guys. Now he looked over at us and asked, "Ready to go?"

"Sure," Crane said.

Mr. Grayle looked at me. I nodded. He winked at me. It was kind of dorky, but I winked back anyway.

"Annie Hoffman, testing for Berry Calvin, *Country Day*, take One," the cameraman said. Then he pulled out an actual black-and-white clapper thing and clapped the sticks together.

The first line was Jody's.

"Aren't you that freshman?" Crane asked.

My mouth was dry. We had lights, camera, and now I was letting the team down with action.

"Depends what you mean by 'that freshman,' " I managed, sounding more than a little shaky.

"The one who was in the middle of the food fight today."

I felt my shoulders shrug automatically. "Probably someone else."

"Probably not," Crane/Jody shot back.

"Look, why does it matter to you?" When I'd rehearsed with Aunt Alexandra, that line had come out sounding sort of tired and yielding. Now, it sounded more accusatory. Prickly, even. Maybe I was responding to Crane's cocky Jody Holt–ness.

"Curiosity," he answered.

"Yeah, well, killed the cat," I replied, tossing my hair a little. I wasn't normally a hair tosser and I hadn't meant to do it. It had just seemed completely unavoidable. I stared at Crane's perfect, glowing skin and felt myself melting at the perfection of it but also a little jealous.

"Where are you from?" Crane asked. "You've got a southern accent."

"I do *not*!"

And in that second, I surrendered, hopelessly and completely, into my fate. I *was* Berry Calvin.

chapter 9

"Mom? I'm glad I caught you at home," I said into the telephone.

"Annie! Sweetheart, I'm so glad you called." Mom sounded thrilled to hear from me. Across the table from me, Gilbert Grayle looked anxious. I gave him a thumbs-up sign.

"I'm glad I called, too. I, um, I have some pretty wild news."

"Did you get your eyebrow pierced?"

How'd she know I wanted to do that? Sometimes my mother borders on psychic.

"Very funny." I rolled my eyes at Gilbert and Aunt Alexandra. "No extra piercings, I promise. But this is really crazy. There's this TV producer and he lives in Aunt Alexandra's building and I met him and he thought I'd be really perfect for this new show he's doing."

"Wow, how flattering," Mom said. I could hear her typing something in the background. Maybe, since she wasn't paying attention, I could somehow slip this through.

"Yeah, it was, except the part is for this sort of dorky fourteen-year-old violinist."

"Well, he must have asked because he overheard you playing the violin."

"Or casting hadn't sent over enough authentically dorky girls," I said more honestly. "Anyway, I auditioned and they want me to be in the show."

The typing stopped.

"I think I missed something," Mom said.

"Gilbert Grayle, this TV producer who lives in Aunt Alexandra's building, wants me to be in a TV show," I repeated patiently.

"Say it again."

"Jeez, Mom, I got a part in a TV show. It's called *Country Day*." There was silence.

"Want me to repeat it again?" I offered.

"No, I think I got it this time."

There was a silence. Gilbert made a move toward the phone. I shook my head at him.

"It's legitimate, I promise," I explained, trying to fill in some details. "I know you're thinking that I fell for some smooth-talking New York con man, but I didn't. This is real. I had an audition at the network—it's Spider Broadcasting—and Aunt Alexandra came with me and I got the part and they want me to sign a contract."

"Alexandra took you?" Mom said.

"Yeah."

"Let me talk with her for a moment." Mom's voice would have liquefied steel. I shrugged and handed Aunt Alexandra the phone.

I regret to say that Mom and Dad were still being what I called "tyrannical" and what they called "concerned" when I flew home on Sunday.

"I could always become an emancipated minor, you know," I said when I greeted them outside airport security.

Mom kissed me. "Let's at least get to the car," she said.

"This is my big chance," I explained for the thousandth time. "Wouldn't you feel guilty depriving me of fame and fortune?"

"I thought you hated this kind of TV show," Dad said flatly. He was carrying my suitcase even though it had wheels.

"OK, I'm not going to be *watching* this show. I'll be in it. That's a totally different experience."

"What if the show gets canceled three weeks into the season?" Mom asked.

"Then I'll be sad and disappointed, but I'll have had a fun experience and lost nothing. Look," I continued, using the best argument I could. "I know you're anxious about this, but I checked your star signs and it's natural that a Taurus like you would feel especially nervous during a lunar cessation. You have to remember this out-of-control feeling is simply illusory and could result in the unfortunate denial of *my* destiny."

"What about school?" Dad changed the topic.

"They'll give me a tutor. Gilbert told you about that." Like seventeen times already.

"And violin?"

"It's New York. They have all these famous Russian violin teachers," I answered through my gritted teeth.

"And Meg and Sarah?"

"I can come back to visit."

Nathan tugged at my shirt. "What about me?"

"Don't know, brat, what about you?" I teased.

Mom sighed. Something about the sigh started to sound resigned.

"Look, I don't think you understand what a major opportunity this is," I added. "You guys act like this could happen to anyone. But it can't and it didn't."

"Annie, we understand," Dad began. "But this just seems like a rash choice. I don't know that you really grasp the repercussions of this."

"Give me some credit. I was there. I auditioned. I *met* these people," I snapped, staring at the airport parking lot through a glaze of repressed tears. Why could I not seem to stop crying lately? Maybe there was a biological explanation—like my hormone levels had shot up on my sixteenth birthday, shifting from occasionally irritating to constantly problematic.

"We just want to be sure this is the best choice for you."

"Why can't I make my own choices?" There was no answer. Just to be sure I got the last word in, I added, "You're being *ridiculous.*"

chapter 10

With all the upheaval of my possible new TV career, music camp had been slightly postponed. So I went out with Meg and Sarah the next afternoon. They had to pick me up—given that I was potentially moving to the public transportation paradise of New York, it didn't really seem worth retaking the driving test.

Meg apparently disagreed. She didn't understand why I hadn't woken at dawn and leaped straight from bed, like a kid on Christmas. According to her, my heart should have been pounding with the joy of being able to right such a tremendous and tragic event. I should have been in line at the motor vehicle bureau when they opened, enthusiasm radiating from my every pore.

I said, "It's nice to see you again, too."

In a stellar example of teenage driving, Meg turned onto University Boulevard without signaling. My heart rate remained thankfully normal.

"Annie, I just think it's important that you get over this phobia as soon as you can," she explained.

"I'm not phobic," I answered automatically.

"It's sort of like when you throw up. You totally don't want to eat whatever you had right before you puked, but it's really all psychological."

"That analogy," I said primly, "is beyond me." Especially since what I'd had before my last hurl had been a healthy dose of the motor vehicle bureau.

As Meg headed down River Road, I cranked the radio up and thought about how I hadn't known that I hated my life until the possibility to escape it arrived. I guess self-awareness has never been my strong suit. When we circled past a strip mall, I noticed there was a little Indian grocery at the end. "Hey, have you ever been there?" I asked.

"Where?" Meg and Sarah asked simultaneously.

"India Market." I pointed.

"No, you want to go?"

"Yeah."

Inside, it was small and dusty. We were the only ones there. We wandered around, picking up spices and Hindi books and cans of Coke. It was kind of like a general store. They even had shoes.

"We could cook something," Meg said.

"Sure." I looked at the shelves. "What? A lot of this looks kind of complicated."

Sarah grabbed a cylindrical package. "Chapatis," she answered. "It's bread. You just sort of heat it."

"Sure," I said again.

By the time we had gotten back to my house with our package of chapatis, I was ranting about my parents' long list of warnings regarding *Country Day*. In fairness, both Meg and Sarah had already heard this spiel about twelve times and continued to endure it with patience.

"They keep saying that I don't realize what I'm getting into and I'm going to be exposed to all these pressures that I don't even know exist and it'll be hard work and not fun," I said.

Meg was reading the chapati package and simultaneously twirling a hank of dyed black hair around her finger. "We need a frying pan," she answered. Then she added, "What kind of pressures?"

"Who knows?" I slammed the pan down with slightly more force than I'd intended. "Drinking? Maybe drugs? Maybe girls who think you have to wear a ton of makeup and eat nothing but celery all day long?"

"Hello!!!" Meg said. "They should, like, set foot in our school one of these days."

"Tell me about it," I agreed. "OK, it says here that we should heat six inches of vegetable oil." That seemed like a lot of oil, so I poured a more reasonable puddle in the pan.

"At any rate," I continued. "They're being like totally absurd. This is the most important thing that's ever happened to me and they're freaking out about the fact that I'll be getting special tutoring with these other kids instead of being incarcerated in Bryant High."

"So?" Meg threw two chapatis in the pan. "That's a godsend as far as I'm concerned."

"It's so clear that your parents are threatened by your entry into a domain that feels foreign to them," Sarah threw in. "I mean, it's New York. It's all the stuff that your parents turned their backs on when they moved to Alabama."

"So? That was their choice and this is mine."

"Uh-oh," Meg said. "Do you think it's supposed to be doing that?" She pointed at the chapati pan, which was suddenly issuing huge clouds of black smoke.

"Probably not." I went over to the pan. The chapatis had shriveled to two black and papery disks. "Hey, come here."

It happened before Meg even got to the stove. The pan— literally—burst into flames.

"Spontaneous combustion!" I shrieked.

Nathan wandered into the kitchen. "What's going on?"

I lost it.

"Get out! Get out get out get out, or I will sell you to the child slave trade," I yelled.

"Annie, the kitchen is on fire," he said.

Duh.

"Get out!" I screamed again.

He did. Meg, by then, had found a box of baking soda, which

she dumped on the frying pan. The flames shrank into a grayish, chalky, bubbling pile.

We all gasped in relief.

"OK, like, imagine if I had died in a kitchen fire right before my first day of *Country Day*," I said, moving the pan to the sink. The baking soda–chapati pile burped at me.

Meg snickered. "Hardly a Hollywood ending."

chapter 11

Naturally, my parents knew about the chapati incident before they even set foot in the door because Nathan ran out of the house, screaming, "Annie set the kitchen on fire!"

(Incidentally, I have since looked up child slavery on the Internet. It turns out that there is this really big problem with child exploitation on cocoa farms in the Ivory Coast. I'm sure that I should find this morally reprehensible, but enslaving Nathan so that he can increase the world's chocolate production frankly seems like an *excellent* idea.)

That night, my dad said in a serious, sober voice, "Annie, did you start the fire in the kitchen because we were fighting about *Country Day*?"

I couldn't help it. I laughed.

"Forget I asked," Dad said.

"Um, yes," I managed between giggles. "Definitely. And if you don't let me move to New York, the violence is going to escalate."

"Thanks for the warning." Dad sounded faintly disgusted.

I had been slouching on the couch, but now I sat up straighter. "Look, I know you're worried about me. But, honestly, it's silly. There's no guarantee that *Country Day* is going to be an unhealthier atmosphere than Bryant High. And, you know what? Give me some credit. I've not succumbed to peer pressure yet. I really don't think I have that kind of personality. Plus . . ." I stopped.

"Plus what?"

"Plus nothing cool has ever happened to me. All I do is wake up, go to school, play the violin, and go to sleep. And it's not like that's a bad life. But this is my chance to do something really extraordinary and exciting. If I were six, I could see you being worried. But I'm *sixteen*. I'll be out of the nest in two years anyway. But by that time *Country Day* will have found another Berry. Chances like this are so, so, so rare, and if I don't jump on it, I may never have anything like this happen to me again."

"You've never acted. Are you sure you'll be able to do it?"

"Well, yeah, that's true. But they want me for Berry because I'm like her. It's typecasting. And I think it's sort of neat that they want someone like me to be on a TV show."

There was a pause.

"I hope you'll never be out of the nest completely," Dad said. "But you're right: This is a neat opportunity. So your mom and I stopped off on the way home and got you a little present for when you move to the city."

I felt a little dizzy. "Really?" I breathed. "I can go?"

Dad nodded. "We'll make arrangements to sign the contracts first thing in the morning."

"Thank you!" I flung my arms around him. Then I remembered the present. "Hey, what'd you get me?"

Dad handed me a small canister on a key ring. I stared at it. "Mace??!!"

Dad shrugged. "It's dangerous in New York."

In other words . . . you can take the girl out of the nest, but you can't take the nest out of the girl.

The day before I was supposed to leave, *The Tuscaloosa News* ran a big story on me. The first line was "Sixteen is sweet for former Bryant High School student Annie Hoffman." That was

OK. The part that was not OK was line 17: "Until *Country Day* came into the picture, Annie's biggest worry was whether or not she would pass the driving test on her second try."

I am going to sue. Because of having to sign a contract, I now have a lawyer, and I have every intention of putting him to good use. Mom pointed out that this couldn't exactly count as slander, since slander has to be false and I honestly didn't pass the driving test. But I still think I have a legitimate case because passing the driving test was never my biggest worry. What I was most worried about was the entirety of my high school finding out—which, thanks to the loudmouth *News,* has now become reality.

(I am therefore relieved to be moving to a city where the standards of "all the news that's fit to print" exist.)

I got an e-mail later that day.

> Annie, oh my goodness! That is so cool about you and TV!!! I guess this means you won't be at school this year. We'll miss you ☺
> Isn't it funny that they picked you because you fit the part for the show?
> Let me know if you ever need a TV sister. We kind of look alike, you know.
> At any rate, congratulations!!!!
> Friends forever (I hope!)
> Sharon Roberts

Sharon Roberts is one of the prettiest girls at school. I look like Sharon the way a dandelion looks like a gladiola (i.e., perhaps part of the same phylum). Since I only talk to her about once a decade, I was pretty disgusted by the phoniness.

Meg was even more appalled. "Annie, if I can't move to New York with you, don't expect me to be here when you return. It's entirely possible that I'll asphyxiate from an overdose of bootlicking."

My mother smiled indulgently at this statement. My whole family had gone out to dinner with Meg and Sarah as a little good-bye party. I had noticed people looking at us. It was either because they had seen the newspaper article or because Nathan was repeatedly (and, thank goodness, silently) enacting "you must pay the rent" with his napkin. My parents had yet to say anything to him about this.

"I'm sure Sharon meant to be nice," Mom said.

I made a face. "I'm sure Sharon meant to camouflage her obvious jealousy," I said, mimicking Mom's tone of voice perfectly. Then I reached across the table for the bread basket.

Sarah giggled. "What's the first thing you're going to do when you get to New York?" she asked.

"Get my eyebrow pierced."

"Awesome."

"Really?" Nathan stopped his napkin antics.

"Yup. They actually changed the character. Berry's now a punk."

Meg snorted. "She's a skinhead."

"A juvie."

"She plays the violin—but she plays Marilyn Manson on it."

"She has 'lust' tattooed across her lip."

"Which, of course, is pretty, but not glamorous."

We were laughing, all of us, even my parents.

"It's required by contract that I dye my hair black," I added.

"Fishnets with the school uniform, of course," Sarah finished, just as the waitress brought our dinner.

After she left, I looked at my parents. "She forgot the celebratory champagne."

"We're saving it for the after-party," Mom said. I noticed she had tears in her eyes. From laughing?

"Mom?" I asked.

"Mm-hm," she answered, dabbing unsubtly at her eyes with the sleeve of her cardigan.

"Are you, like, crying?"

"Oh, sweetie, we're going to miss you so much," she said in this weird, choky after-school-special kind of voice.

And that was it. I could feel myself starting to mist up and my dinner suddenly tasted like Styrofoam and I stared at the table in silence.

The knowledge came in a flash, an absolute avalanche of revelations. I had been horribly, horribly wrong. I didn't want to go to New York and spend all day pretending to be someone else. This had all been a mistake. I don't even like getting my *picture* taken; how on earth could I parade in front of a TV camera for eight hours a day? It would have been far more gracious to decline the whole invitation and stay in Tuscaloosa with Meg and Sarah whining about how nothing exciting ever happened to me.

It might be babyish or wimpy—but I just wasn't as ready to hop the nest as I had so brazenly advertised. How could I have ever thought that being alone, in a big dirty city, with only six-foot-tall glamazons for company, was preferable to my cozy life? I would even miss Nathan and his monster snot.

"Annie? Annie!" Mom was calling my name. "I didn't mean to upset you."

"Oh, don't worry about it," I answered, staring at the table before me. "It's no big deal. It's just that—like the proverbial drowning man—I saw my whole life flash before my eyes and realized it hasn't been so bad after all."

Meg grinned across the table at me.

"Like, wow, Annie," she said. "How deep."

chapter 12

This time when the plane landed at LaGuardia, I walked briskly down to Baggage Claim, where Gilbert Grayle said a driver would meet me. As soon as I got through baggage claim, there was a man with walrus mustache holding a big sign that had "A. Hoffman" written on it in black marker.

(The walrus-mustache driver then proceeded to spend the entire trip name-dropping about previous passengers. Like I care that Frankie Muniz's butt once graced my seat. I was obviously a total waste of a day for this guy: It's not like tomorrow's glamorous traveler would find it fascinating that he drove Annie Hoffman.)

Spider Broadcasting wasn't giving me a lot of time to settle into my new home. Rather than going to Aunt Alexandra's, the driver took me directly to the network building, where this seven-foot-tall blond woman whisked me upstairs to meet my fellow cast members.

"You're the last one to arrive!" she exclaimed. "I cannot tell you how excited we are to have you as Berry. I mean, look at you." She reached out and fingered the sleeve of my striped T-shirt. "You *are* Berry."

I crossed my fingers and offered up a silent prayer that I would not hyperventilate in the elevator and have to be revived with a cold bucket of water in front of the entire exquisite, untypecast cast. In the history of truly idiotic ideas, my agreeing to play Berry ranked somewhere between Diet Coke Twist and Hannibal leading elephants over the Alps. I mean, was it possible

I'd been hypnotized this whole time and was just now coming out of the trance?

The elevator stopped.

Noooooooo.

"Here we are!" my guide said brightly.

I emitted a feeble little groan that I hoped would suffice for a reply and slowly followed her down the hall. She stopped in front of a closed door. "They're right in here. Just go on in."

"Mmm-uuuh," I grumble-moaned in terrified agreement. Then I counted to three-Mississippi and opened the door. This was just one small step for geek and one large step for geek-kind.

For a second, no one noticed I was there. There was a long meeting table in the middle of the room. No one was sitting at the table, unless you counted Crane Renfrew, who was perched on top of the table, lounging backward like he was in a beach chair and generally reveling in his own fabulousness. He was talking to a tall, dark-haired girl. Then he spotted me and let out a wolf whistle. The entire room of mingling people swiveled toward me. In three seconds, Crane Renfrew had gone from beautiful to satanic.

"Annie Hoffman, everyone," he said.

I smiled weakly and stumbled toward the table. The throng of people parted slightly to let me through. I could feel the foolish smile still plastered on my face.

When I sat down, next to Crane's swinging leg, Gilbert Grayle materialized beside me.

"May as well get started," he announced. Squeezing my shoulder, he leaned down and murmured, "Would you like anything? A drink?"

Now might be a good time for my first-ever martini.

"Um, sure, a Coke," I said aloud. "Thanks."

Gilbert reached over to a table on the wall and plucked a can of Coke from a big ice bucket. When I opened it, the hiss seemed very loud.

"This is it, everyone," Gilbert said. "Welcome to *Country Day.*"

The room erupted into cheers.

"In this room, right now, we have the future of television's number-one show."

More cheers. Crane let out another wolf whistle.

"Our writing team has crafted one heck of a series premiere." Gilbert gestured toward two men and a woman, all wearing black and sipping mineral water. One of the men opened a box on the floor beside him and began passing binders of scripts around the table. I opened mine.

Country Day

Episode 1:

What I Did on My Summer Vacation

A small shiver of excitement began somewhere in the pit of my stomach. This was a hundred times cooler than Juilliard and about a billion times cooler than Bryant High.

Gilbert said something that I missed that triggered more cat-calls and cheers. Happily, I joined in with everyone else.

"This is a cast like nothing I have ever seen before," he beamed. "Crane Renfrew, you were born to play Jody Holt." Crane stood up and gave a lazy wave, as though the entire room hadn't already been aware of his magnetically golden presence and shrilly brilliant whistling.

"Hallie Masterson as Kit Winters." The tall, dark girl next to Crane stood up and smiled. If she was sixteen, then I was two.

"Katrina Rocco and Frank Murphy as the most neglectful parents I've ever seen." This was greeted by laughter.

"A young lady about whom we are very hopeful," Gilbert said, winking at me. "Friends, Annie Hoffman as Berry Calvin."

As soon as he said that, I stopped being nervous. Like Crane and Hallie, I stood up, smiled, and gave a slow, languid wave.

Yes, Annie, this is your life.

Later that day, after about a billion publicity photos, I finally got to Aunt Alexandra's. One extra perk of *Country Day* was this whole driver thing. If I could only keep up the fame charade, I might never have to submit myself to the driver's seat again.

Through a feat of incredible persuasion, I talked Aunt Alexandra into Thai food for dinner. One bizarre thing about Aunt Alexandra is that she likes all the food on her plate to be about the same color. Like Dover sole and rice and mashed potatoes (ew) or rare steak with tomato salad. Thai food almost always mixes up a bunch of different-colored vegetables. I took it as a sign of just how well we were going to get along that she was willing to sacrifice psychological tranquility for my ethnic food addiction.

Meg called my new cell phone halfway through my Pad Basil and Aunt Alexandra's Pad Thai with everything worthwhile picked out. Aunt Alexandra let out a little half gasp.

"What's that?"

"Cell phone," I muttered, rummaging through my bag. "Meggie!" I shrieked into the phone.

"*Why* on earth do you have that?" Aunt Alexandra asked.

"There's a big photo of you up in the drama classroom," Meg said.

"My parents want me on an electronic leash," I told Aunt Alexandra. "That's the grossest thing I ever heard," I answered Meg. Aunt Alexandra thought I was still talking to her.

"It's ludicrous," she responded.

"I know," said Meg. "I tried to take it down, but Mrs. Chan caught me."

"We've got to get rid of it," I squeaked.

"Yes, get rid of it. I'll tell your parents that it is unacceptable!" Aunt Alexandra exclaimed. "To say nothing of rude, interrupting dinner conversation as it does."

"Unacceptable," I repeated.

"Unacceptable," Meg echoed.

"You are almost an adult," said Aunt Alexandra.

"Look, I agree," I answered them both. "Everyone is making way too big a deal out of this TV show. I'm still *me*."

There was a beeping.

"Hang on; I have another call."

"Annie!" Meg said.

"Another?" Aunt Alexandra looked as thought she might possibly be having a coronary. I really wished they had vodka gimlets at Lemongrass Grill.

"Annie, we've been leaving messages all day," Mom said. "We didn't even know if you got in safely."

Oops. I *had* promised to call.

"Sorry, I forgot," I apologized. "It's been a crazy day. This chauffeur picked me up from the airport and I had all this TV stuff, so I guess I just got caught up."

"A chauffeur?" said Mom.

"Of course you had a chauffeur," Aunt Alexandra drawled, unimpressed.

"You have to tell Nathan." I remembered Meg. "Wait five seconds, Mom." I clicked back.

"Can I call you back? My public is awaiting me."

Forget drinking gimlets. Aunt Alexandra was turning into one. Her skin had taken on the same unmistakable chartreuse hue.

"OK, I cannot deal with you being a star," Meg answered.

Join the club, Meg. Join the club.

chapter 13

The night before the first day of filming, I didn't sleep. At all. I mean, it's possible that I may have closed my eyes for about thirty seconds between 3:00 and 4:00 A.M., but it's not as if any productive rest occurred. When the alarm sounded, I had been staring at a crack in the ceiling for about an hour. I had never noticed the crack before, but it seemed very likely that the entire roof of the apartment was going to shatter and I would be suffocated by moldy Sheetrock and deprived of my chance at fame and fortune. I could almost hear Meg as she paraded past my coffin, wearing a phenomenal broad-rimmed black hat.

"Whoa," she'd hiss to Sarah. "I had no idea Annie was so into that raccoon-eyed exhausted-waif look."

At any rate, *Country Day* had asked that we be on-set at the remarkably cruel hour of 7:00 A.M. So it was 5:30 when I stepped into the shower. I was pretty sure I'd never been willingly conscious at 5:30 before. But for the next hour, I did all the necessary primping which I usually skimp on. I shaved my legs. I exfoliated. I put some blue pore-refining gloop that Sarah had given me on my face and endured five intense minutes of tingling. I knew that everything I did would all be redone before filming. But I could hardly show up for my first official day as a TV star looking anything less than sparkling. So, when I peeked into Aunt Alexandra's room to say good-bye, I had on a full face of makeup, shiny hair pulled back into a low ponytail, and my absolute most knock-dead jeans. Aunt Alexandra was snoring softly with an eye mask over her eyes. Rather than disturb her, I left a note on the nightstand:

> Off to face my destiny and greet my public. See you for dinner tonight.
>
> Maybe Café Jacques?
>
> xxxxxxx,
> Annie

In the lobby, I waved good-bye to the doorman. (Unfortunately not Jules. He doesn't come on duty till 9:00.) Spider had promised me they would send a car for me and, sure enough, there was a Lincoln Town Car waiting. As soon as I stepped onto the curb, a guy jumped out of the front seat.

"Ms. Hoffman?" He wasn't wearing a uniform or a peaked cap or anything like that, just a dark suit, but I felt very *Lifestyles of the Rich and Famous* anyway.

"Yeah, hi," I answered. He opened the door with a flourish and I collapsed into the leather interior. There was a copy of the *Times* waiting on the seat. A small box was attached to the back of the front seat. I opened it. Inside was a selection of juices and fruit. In the interest of continuing the charade of Annie's poshness, I selected blueberry-pomegranate.

The driver slid open the Plexiglas panel dividing the front seat from the back. "Filming is in Long Island City, in Queens," he said as we sped down Broadway. "Should take about half an hour at this time of day."

I nodded and began flipping through the paper.

"My name is Jeremiah. I'll be your regular driver. If there's anything you'd want for your ride that I didn't provide today, just let me know."

Was he kidding? If it weren't too early, I would call Meg and start cawing about how there was *blueberry-pomegranate juice in my car refrigerator*. Aloud, I said, "I'm sure I'll be fine."

A few minutes and a lot of newsprint later, I realized my mistake. I knocked on the privacy panel and Jeremiah slid it open.

"Um, actually," I said timidly. "If it's not too much trouble, I'd love a paper with a horoscope."

I had no idea what I expected the set to be like, but somehow I had never exactly pictured myself sauntering into what appeared to be a large airplane hangar. The street outside was kind of grimy. It was a major comedown from the chauffeured car, definitely not star quality. Inside, it was total chaos, with people rushing around with headsets and large metal cranes and big speakers.

"Hi," I said to no one in particular. When nothing happened, I repeated myself a little more loudly.

Nothing. After a few more moments of standing around, I reached out and touched one of the rushing people as she whizzed past me. She spun around with an irritated look.

"We need to get the kliegs up," she snapped.

"Oh." I felt dumb, even though I knew I'd done nothing wrong. "I'm Annie. I'm supposed to be here for filming."

"Are you a PA? Check in with Dwayne. Assistants were supposed to be here an hour ago." She started to walk away.

"No," I called after her. "I'm in the show." She kept walking. "I play Berry Calvin," I finished lamely.

"You're Annie?" A tall guy with a shaved head stopped in front of me. "You're supposed to be in makeup."

"Which is where?" I asked.

"Come on." He began weaving through the headsetted crowd. "You should come around the side from now on." He led me out of the airplane hangar. Silently, we walked down the long cement expanse to the back of the building, where I could see rows of white trailers. They looked like the "portables" where we had class when my elementary school was being re-modeled. My guide stopped in front of one. "That's makeup. You come here first every day."

"OK."

He pointed to another portable. "That's your trailer. You can hang out there or whatever you want between takes."

"OK," I said again, feeling sort of helpless. If I'd only been able to read my horoscope this morning, I would have been forewarned for general bafflement. Instead, I was walking into the single most important day of my destiny astrologically unprepared.

As my guide vanished back into the world of busy black-clad people with headsets, I knocked on the door of the makeup trailer. It flew open.

"Hey," a voice drawled. It was Max, the guy who'd done my face for my audition. "We've been waiting for you."

Inside, the trailer looked kind of like the inside of a hair sa-lon, all mirrors and black chairs and filled with chemically fruity smells. I saw Hallie and Frank Murphy sitting in the chairs. A woman in a green smock stood over Hallie with tweezers. Frank's face was smeared with something white.

I followed Max to a chair. There was a big bouquet of flow-ers standing on the counter.

"Are those for me?" I asked curiously, settling into the chair.

"Who else?" Max handed me the card. I opened it.

> Welcome, Annie!
> With warmest regards from Spider Broadcasting

Automatically, I found myself thinking nice, warm, fuzzy thoughts about Spider Broadcasting. Happily, I glanced up at Max.

"Don't get too settled," he told me. "You need to go get your hair washed before anything else."

"I just washed it an hour ago," I said, forgetting that I hadn't wanted to admit how much time I'd spent on my appearance. It was obviously a good thing that the vast majority of what came out of my mouth for the rest of the day was going to be scripted. My lips were simply untrustworthy.

"Hair is right there," Max said, pointing to the end of the room. I unsettled myself and walked to where he pointed. A woman with lots of curly hair piled on top of her head smiled at me.

"Sit down here," she ordered, whisking a copper-colored smock around my shoulders and snapping it up with efficient fingers. "Tilt back." I did. A rush of warm water flooded over my head. "You come here first every day. You can have anyone who's available wash your hair, but you want me or Quita," she pointed to a woman encased entirely in turquoise leather, "to style it."

The hair wash was proving to be the most luxurious scalp massage of my life. I closed my eyes and attempted to relax.

Attempted would be the operative word.

chapter 14

The word *stellar* comes from the Latin word *stella,* which means "star." It's the first declension, which is pretty much the first thing you learn when you start taking Latin. I would just like to note that an hour after I arrived in the *Country Day* makeup trailer, I looked stellar in the most starry, glittering, enviable sense of the word. I had thought I looked decently stellar when I sauntered out of Aunt Alexandra's apartment at quarter to dawn that morning. But, in fact, I had been very wonderfully wrong.

Here is what I think. Stars *don't* look like everyone else; lots of them really do have more perfect features and alluring eyes and chiselly cheekbones. Hallie, for example, almost looked worse after makeup, because she's so naturally glowing that her delicate perfection was sort of drowned by it all.

On the other hand, someone like me—someone sort of vaguely pretty in an entirely ordinary way—looked truly sensational after the whole colossal shebang of three fluttering people and products derived from the essential oils of rare Tanzanian botanicals. I still didn't look like Hallie, but the gap between us had shrunk a good bit.

The hair person—her name turned out to be Shira—returned me to Max with my hair so glossy that you could practically see your reflection in it. I'd always thought my long brown hair sort of boring, but the sudden gleam made me reconsider. Max tied it back with a soft cloth and set to work on my face, chattering so quickly that I could barely understand him.

"Darling, it's so good to see you here. We'll have you looking beautiful. Casting didn't know what they were doing; thank God Gilbert stepped in; none of those other girls were as inherently Berry as you. They were just so sophisticated and confident; you've got just the right presence and you'll do fabulously. You've got your lines memorized, right? Course you do. Now this is a mask we're going to use every day on you. It's got a bit of fruit acid, which will even your complexion right out. I want you to use this at home also."

With the mask smeared inelegantly across my face, Max dropped the chair back and set to work with tweezers on my brows.

"Just a little touch-up here. You know, darling, the right brow can really change a face so much. We did a little for the audition, but now it's time to get them straight."

The pain of tweezing was unexpectedly intense. "Mmmppph," I cried out, but stiffening layers of mask made it difficult for me to talk. I heard a tinkling laugh. It was Hallie Masterson, standing beside Max.

"You'll get used to it," she said comfortingly. "I promise."

My breath was coming out in heaving gasps. "Are you almost done?" I whispered after what seemed like a tremendously long time.

"Don't talk," Max ordered. "It changes the shape of your face."

I wondered if anyone had ever fainted during brow shaping and, if so, if being *unconscious* changed the shape of the face.

At last, Max flicked the tweezers back onto a shelf and began sponging the mask off my face delicately. Tears started streaming from my eyes. He flipped the chair up.

"Now, isn't that better?" he demanded. As the region around my eyes was now a flaming fuchsia, I did not see the massive improvement. But I just smiled weakly and said nothing.

After tweezing, Max steamed, exfoliated, and moisturized my face. I worried that my glossy hair might get frizzy, but when I mentioned this he just laughed and said that Shira knew better than that. A full hour after I'd entered the makeup trailer, he finally pulled out the actual makeup. Squirting a creamy orange paste from a tube onto his fingers, he began patting it over my face.

"Isn't this kind of dark for me?" I asked. I have very pale skin. It's olive toned, but fair olive, if that makes sense. With the foundation on, I looked like one of those Gauguin paintings of Tahiti, where all the women are unnaturally beige.

"The camera will wash you out otherwise. We use it for everyone." Max reached for a silver case full of brushes and pulled out three. "Close your eyes."

"Are you using three brushes just for my eyes?"

"Maybe four. Depends. Wardrobe says you're wearing blue today, which I personally wouldn't do for you, but that's hardly my job." The brush tickled as it dabbed across my eyelid. "OK, you can open."

A stranger with carroty skin stared back at me. The eyes popped luminously from her face. They were beckoning eyes, the eyes of an interesting, intelligent person, someone you'd want to know. With a thicker brush, Max began sweeping blush over me. In a few minutes, I had the cheekbones to match the eyes. He began filling in my lips with a pencil that seemed the exact same color of my skin. Slowly, he added a shiny pink gloss and then a browner gloss.

"What do you think, darling?" he asked, setting the lip brush back into the silver case.

"Except for the fact that I'm orange," I began honestly, "I look, well, kind of amazing. Like, if I weren't me, I would totally want to get to know me."

Max grinned. "I know," he said. "I'm a genius. Now let's pop you off to your trailer. You need to change. You're on-camera in twenty minutes."

I'd been enjoying playing princess until Max said that. But all of a sudden I remembered that this attention came at the cost of convincing everyone I deserved to be a fancy TV star. Slowly, I left makeup and found my trailer. It was really nice inside, with more fresh flowers and a big comfy couch with colorful throw pillows. I couldn't believe someone had picked out this furniture just for me. There was a metal rack, the kind they have at any normal department store or at the Gap, with clothes hung on it. Each outfit was sheathed in plastic, with a note pinned to the outside. The first note said: "Scene 1, principal's office." Underneath the plastic was a very simple slate blue linen dress with buttons down the front. I had hoped for clothes to match my fabulous face, but this was kind of, well, honestly? It was frumpy.

There was a knock on the door. "Five minutes," a voice called. Quickly I stepped out of my jeans and into the dress. I turned to the mirror. The wardrobe department had taken tons of measurements of me last week. I'd been wrong. This dress was frumpy the way a leather bustier is frumpy. Sure, it was simple, but it also hugged the curves I didn't really possess and managed to be both modest and sexy at the same time. I would gladly have worn it every remaining second of my life.

With a deep breath, I stepped out of the trailer and into the spotlight.

chapter 15

Highlights, apparently, equal high life. After two days on-set, I established that I was pretty much the only person working on *Country Day* who did not use color shampoo. This included Joey the sound guy and the woman who restocked the minifridges in the trailers. So, in the interest of approximating city-slicker chic-dom, I bought some of Hallie's favorite obscure Israeli brand and went back to Aunt Alexandra's to experiment.

The shampoo turned out to be as thick as toothpaste and extremely red. According to the saleslady, it would enhance my hidden auburn tones. Gamely I stepped into the shower and raked a healthy amount through my hair. Almost immediately ruby rivers began coursing down my skin and onto the shower floor. After a few minutes, when the red stream failed to lessen, I began to worry. I get enough serenades of "Tomorrow" just being named Annie. If my hair actually turned the color of Little Orphan Annie's, Hallie Masterson and I were going to have serious words.

There was a sudden banging on the door. I ignored it. Bang. Bang.

"Anna Claire Hoffman!" Aunt Alexandra's pounding took on a slightly desperate quality.

I turned down the stream of water and screeched back at her, "What?" Unnecessarily, I added, "I'm taking a shower."

Aunt Alexandra pounded and screamed something unintelligible back at me.

"I can't hear you," I yelled, and turned the water back up. My skin was turning an ominous shade of pink.

"Your tutor is here."

Oh no. Oh *no!* How on earth had it slipped my mind that this was the first afternoon of my "guided study" program? My tutor was here and I was stuck in something that looked like the shower scene out of *Psycho.*

"Be right there."

Ten minutes later, I emerged. The shower still looked like *Psycho.* The snowy white bath mat was a splotchy pink. My face had been dyed a color that I hoped could be described as a healthy flush. My scalp was flaming fuchsia. But my hair was— as always—brown. As far as I could tell, Hallie's magical Israeli highlighter had had absolutely no effect on my persistently blah hair.

Grand.

Wet-headed, I made my way into Aunt Alexandra's living room. To eliminate the possibility that I might become over-stressed and have to enter a hospital for exhaustion like virtually every other teen star, my tutor was supposed to work with me at home fifteen hours a week. I personally could not imagine how we were going to fit a normal high school curriculum into that time, but it seemed in my best interests to smile and go along with it. Meg and I had agreed that the tutor was probably going to be a middle-aged woman with a plummy British accent, a cat named Agatha, and a fondness for the Brontë sisters.

In the living room, I found a dark-haired guy wearing cargo shorts and a really beat-up *Rolling Stones* T-shirt. He couldn't have been older than twenty-one.

"Hi," I said. "I'm Annie."

"Cool," the guy answered. "Jason."

"Are you my tutor?"

"Natch."

Awesome. I loved Spider Broadcasting. They clearly had my best interests at heart.

"Let's get started," Jason said. "Is there a better place we can work? Maybe someplace with a desk or table?"

"Kitchen?" I asked.

"That'll do."

Once we were settled at the table with Cokes and a bag of Doritos, Jason began quizzing me about my classes at Bryant High.

"I understand that keeping up Latin is a necessity," he said. "How much Vergil have you translated?"

"Vergil?" A drop of water slid off my hair and onto the spiral notebook in front of me. It left a pink stain. I flipped the page before Jason could notice.

"I thought we could try the *Aeneid*, which is part of the AP requirement," he continued.

"You know Latin?"

Jason looked surprised. He shook his skater-length bangs out of his face.

"Annie, I'm getting a Ph.D. in classics. This is just a part-time job for me."

Oh. I could feel myself blush. Maybe it wasn't noticeable with my new, dyed-pink face.

"It's really a favor to my uncle. He's a bigwig over at Spider."

Double-oh.

"I talked to your parents and we agreed that it made sense to drop bio in order to allow more violin practice." He talked to my *parents?* Jason must know his stuff; otherwise there was no way they'd have been OK with Dogtown tutoring Z-Girl.

Aloud, I asked, "Really?" I could honestly hear the "Hallelujah Chorus" ringing around me. I despise biology; it's all organs and formaldehyde and reproductive cycles of fungus.

Jason grinned. "Yeah. We're substituting one afternoon of more advanced chemistry each week."

The hallelujah choir stopped abruptly.

"And I thought we could choose the literature we wanted to do together." He passed me a list of books and I bent over it. *Franny and Zooey, On the Road, The Bell Jar.* Another splash of pink water trickled off my hair and onto the page. This time Jason noticed.

"Why is your head dripping pink?"

"Umm," I mumbled.

"And your shirt! Oh, jeez."

"What?"

"It's all stained." He tugged the back of my shirt over my shoulder so that I could see the rosy blotches.

"Oh, um," I said unhelpfully.

"What's in your hair?"

I was one long blush, head to foot. Maybe a merciful lightning bolt would put me out of my misery. Like, say, immediately.

"Just shampoo," I muttered.

Jason leaned closer to me. "Your scalp is all red."

"Yeah, I know. You should see the shower. It looks like *Psycho,*" I shot back.

Jason laughed. "Come on." He pulled gently on my arm and I reluctantly stood up. Still holding my elbow, he led me over to the kitchen sink. "Head down," he ordered.

"Jason," I protested faintly. He tapped my hair, which had left a trail of pink across the kitchen tile, and I obediently bent my head into the sink. Berry Calvin may be a dork, but I was absolutely positive that there would never be a *Country Day* episode where she had her hair washed by her tutor. "It was color shampoo," I added defensively.

"Rinse for a second," Jason said. He sounded like he might be laughing. "You look like you have a bad case of flesh-eating bacteria in your hair."

Lovely.

"Why did you do this again?" he asked when he returned from finding normal shampoo.

"Well, everyone at *Country Day* uses color shampoo," I said.

His Pantene-laden fingers made strong circles in my hair. "And if everyone at *Country Day* jumped off a cliff, would you jump, too?"

What an original comment. "It's supposed to bring out my auburn highlights," I answered defensively.

"I don't think it worked."

"I figured that out."

"Solves one problem for us though," he said, rinsing my hair in lukewarm water.

"Which is?"

"What books we're going to read." He squeezed another blob of shampoo into my hair and began rubbing again. "Would you rather start with *A Study in Scarlet* or *The Red Badge of Courage*?"

Oh, ha.

chapter 16

Hallie Masterson decided to have a party to celebrate our first week of filming. I had hoped to spend a long time agonizing on the phone with Meg about what to wear, but she kept suggesting my Bryant High School Physical Education Program shorts. Those things are single-handedly responsible for expanding the hole in the ozone by about three hundred feet (and thereby endangering the papery thin skin of various rare breeds of South American bird). I'd burn mine, except I'm afraid they might liquefy with exposure to heat.

Since Meg was so unhelpful, I was forced to put on a fashion show in the lobby for Jules. He seemed to think that I should wear a skirt.

"That's not too dressy?" I asked, lolling against the front door in my favorite thrift-shop jeans. Regular contact with Jules had done nothing to diminish my crush on him. My throbbing heart was pretty much permanently unstilled.

Jules rolled his eyes in a full 360-degree circle, which meant that I ended up coasting downtown in a little yellow and white dress. No sense not living up to the PollyAnnie stereotype I'd somehow created for myself.

Hallie lived almost on the Hudson River, in a neighborhood I'd never been to before. The doorman double-checked that I was on her party list before telling me to go to Apartment 20-C. I felt very grown-up and very, very alone as I made my way into the elevator, my sandals clacking loudly in the empty lobby.

Outside her apartment, I straightened my dress a little, then bit my tongue and rang the doorbell. Nothing happened.

Ring.

Nothing.

Tentatively, I tried the silver knob, and the door swung inward, revealing a roomful of people. I am not exactly what you would call shy, but diving into a teeming swarm of extremely tall and gorgeous New Yorkers was daunting. Sometimes I think that being on *Country Day* is like living in a reverse *Planet of the Apes;* instead of gorillas, the entire population is exquisite.

"Annie!" Hallie swooped down on me. "You came!"

She was wearing jeans. They did not look like they came from a thrift shop and she also had on this silky black shirt that appeared to be trimmed with actual fur, but I still wished I hadn't listened to Jules. I'm just a thousand times more comfortable armored in denim.

"Sure, hi," I said awkwardly. Hallie was holding a martini glass filled with something that looked sort of like apple juice but probably wasn't. "Thanks for inviting me," I added.

"Of course." She flung an arm around my shoulder. "Let me give you a tour." She showed me the big fancy main room and a smaller bedroom.

"Do you live here alone?" I asked, noticing the way her subtly copper highlights glinted in the light. Color shampoo, obviously.

She nodded.

"What about your parents?" I said automatically, then regretted it. I didn't get why it was necessary that I demonstrate my total uncool, Berry Calvin–like qualities at every possible interaction. Hallie laughed a sort of high-pitched laugh.

"They're in Maine, where I grew up. I haven't lived there in five or six years."

"How old are you?" I asked suspiciously.

Hallie laughed her high laugh again. "Twenty-five."

In that case, I guess she was entitled to put whatever non–apple juice substance she wanted into her martini glass. I mean, I knew she didn't exactly look like your normal high schooler. But *twenty-five?* She was playing someone my age exactly and she was almost a decade older. If truth in advertising laws applied to TV dramas, the entire Accutane-addicted population of Bryant High School would heave a collective sigh of relief.

"Oh," I said aloud. It seemed like I was saying "oh" an awful lot now that I was working on *Country Day*. Maybe I should switch vowels and go with "ah" or "eh" instead, which might at least seem Canadian rather than witless.

As Hallie handed me a Coke, I felt hands cover my eyes.

"Guess 'oo?" a shrill cockney voice asked.

"I don't know," I said slowly and deliberately.

"Come on, be a sport." Frank Murphy, Hallie's onscreen dad, swung in front of me. Frank makes a big deal out of channeling Ward Cleaver, probably because on-screen he plays a totally ruthless womanizer and rotten father.

"Got your lines down for next week yet?" He beamed at me.

"Mostly."

This was a lie. After filming for only one week, I had realized that memorizing lines was a deadly and soul-sucking activity, the *Country Day* equivalent of a Harry Potter dementor.

"We're all looking forward to your violin scene."

I smiled noncommittally. I was sort of looking forward to the violin scene, too, mainly because I didn't have to memorize anything for it.

"You been practicing hard with your teacher?"

"Uh, no."

The violin teacher—or lack thereof—was sort of a sore point with me. *Country Day* had claimed they'd find one, and it was especially important because Berry played. But they'd had tons of time and every time I asked, someone was "still working on it." In fact, I'd run into Gilbert in the elevator this morning, and before I could even say hello he'd announced, "Kiddo, we're working on it." I didn't understand why it was so hard. I mean, if they walked over to Juilliard and talked to the kids who'd gotten in, they'd get the names of a whole lot of newly unemployed instructors.

Frank smiled at me. "Don't need to practice?"

"She doesn't have a teacher yet," Hallie broke in. "Don't you ever pay attention on-set, Frank?"

"Listen, little lady," he began.

Hallie and I squealed in unified protest. Frank threw up his arms and moved away from us, mumbling something that I sincerely hoped was an apology.

"Thanks for inviting me," I told Hallie.

She grinned. "Of course."

As Hallie moved on to meet and greet her other guests (few of whom I recognized), I wandered over to the granite island where Hallie had set out drinks and snacks. Crane Renfrew was there, pouring himself a Sprite. He really was very good-looking. In fact, he and Jules were neck and neck for "Unattainable Man Most Likely to Occupy Annie's Thoughts."

"Seems like everyone here is over twenty-one except for you and me," I greeted him.

Crane looked at me. "Oh, I'm over twenty-one. I just don't want to drink."

Were it possible for my heart actually to stop beating, it might have at that moment. Scoop for the tabloids: Boy Next Door Crane Renfrew Actually Recovering Alcoholic.

"It kind of makes me stick out in this environment, but I just don't feel like it right now," he continued.

"Am I the only one of the cast who's actually in high school?" I asked suspiciously. "Everyone is so . . . old."

Crane grinned. "I might rephrase that if I were you. These are people who spend thousands a year on skin care products to make them look younger."

"Did you know I don't have a violin teacher yet?" I changed the topic rather than engage in a conversation about the perpetually gushing fountain of phony youth.

Crane's well-bleached grin expanded a precise millimeter. "Everyone knows that. It bugs you, right?"

"It makes me not feel like me anymore," I confessed. "I haven't learned a new piece in six weeks. I got the sheet music for this Bach concerto that I've always wanted to play, but I needed some help with the timing of the finger work." I paused. "It's not like I'm not nagging everyone about it enough."

Crane refilled my cup and handed it to me.

"One thing you're learning pretty fast is that you have to do whatever it takes to keep your sense of who you are when you're working in TV," he said. "If that's violin for you, then you got to make sure you get your lessons."

I thought about that for a moment and gazed around the glittery room filled with highlighted hair and people who were older than me.

"You know, I think I want to go home," I said.

"Really?"

"Yeah." I came, I saw, and while I didn't technically conquer, I had conquered enough to make me feel like going home to watch Comedy Central was just fine. I smiled radiantly at Crane. "Would you help me find a cab?"

chapter 17

Like Maria von Trapp, I had confidence in confidence alone. Talking to people about my lack of violin lessons at Hallie's party had made me realize just how much I missed them. I liked acting—enough—but I always had to think and stay focused and poised. With the violin, I could forget myself to the point where it was almost like doing nothing at all. So, as soon as I got off filming on Monday, I decided to bag Jason's trig assignment and head to Lincoln Center. After a mere fifteen minutes of aimless wandering, I worked my way over to the administrative offices for Juilliard's high school program.

"Hi," I said to the guy at the front desk. My voice sounded weak and raspy, so I cleared my throat and started over. "Hi. My name's Annie Hoffman. I auditioned for the high school lessons over the summer and didn't get in, but I was hoping that I could either talk to one of the judges or leave a message for her."

The guy looked up slightly from his computer. "Excuse me?"

I repeated myself, as he continued clicking away on his mouse. The pattern of clicks resembled those that might happen in a game of solitaire. Surely an institution as musically advanced as Juilliard provided employees with more vital tasks.

"Why?" he asked, eyes descending back to the screen.

"I need a violin teacher. I hoped she'd have a good suggestion." The fact that I'd barged into Juilliard once before made this whole errand seem, if not exactly sane, a little less ludicrous. "She was tall, with a lot of thick gray hair." The receptionist looked a little blank. "Her bun looked kind of like a ball of yarn."

The receptionist's face cleared. "Helena," he said. "Does she know you?"

"I hoped she might remember me," I said. "She said she liked my playing, and I just moved to New York and I really need a teacher. Please can I leave a note for her?" I begged.

He shrugged.

"Really?" I asked.

He shrugged again. I took this to mean "yes" and pulled out the note that I'd written in my dressing room this morning, while waiting for my five seconds of being filmed walking down the fake high school corridor to my fake locker.

That night, after a dinner of salmon and carrots (which Aunt Alexandra had had delivered, since she obviously would never do anything as radical as turn on the stove), my cell phone rang. I was pretending to do trig problems but mostly staring into the window of the apartment opposite ours, where there was a woman doing something that was either papier-mâché or a big, messy mistake.

"Hello?"

"Is this Annie Hoffman?" The voice was a woman's, but very deep. I had a good feeling about this.

"Yes."

"It's Helena Messer. I believe you left a note for me today."

"You're the judge I met, right?"

There was a pause. "Yes. I remember you."

I grinned into the phone. Houston, we have liftoff!

"I'm curious," she continued. "What are the odd and life-changing circumstances that would bring an Alabama violinist to the big city?"

Breathlessly I explained about getting lost and meeting Gilbert Grayle and my transformation into Berry Calvin. "I couldn't say no. It's the only exciting thing ever to happen to me." There was a pause. "It is really easy to get lost in Lincoln Center," I added.

I had to wait through another pause before Helena spoke. "It is," she agreed. "Would it be the second exciting thing to happen to you if I told you that I'd be happy to take you on as a student?"

I love it when the stars finally align themselves in thoroughly beneficial ways.

"Yes," I gasped into the phone.

"I don't really have time for another student, truthfully. My hope is that you'll be a worthwhile addition."

Me? Worthwhile? But of course . . .

"Thank you," I said aloud. "So much."

"It's fine. Your playing has some qualities worth cultivating."

After we arranged a first meeting, I felt restless. The trig problem set seemed even less exciting than before. I wandered downstairs, but Jules was off-duty and there was a strange (and notably less attractive) doorman at the front desk. So I took the elevator to the seventeenth floor, where Gilbert Grayle lived. I wasn't sure if dropping by unannounced was exactly the kind of thing that neighbors did in New York, but I wanted to tell him about Helena. Besides, we hadn't really gotten a chance to talk since filming started.

Gilbert answered the door in a gray bathrobe. "Annie Hoffman," he announced. "What can I do for you?" He didn't sound unhappy to see me, but neither did he sound overjoyed. It dawned on me that I really didn't know anything about Gilbert's private life.

"I had some good news. I wanted to share."

He held the door open wider and made a come-in motion with his head. I hesitated.

"Let me guess," Gilbert said. "You just finished memorizing next week's script and wanted to tell me how brilliant and realistic the episode was."

I giggled and walked inside. Next week's script was currently lying under a pile of dirty laundry, where I had every intention of leaving it until Sunday night. This was obviously information Gilbert did not need to know. "Is it OK that I came by?"

His apartment was very fancy, but in an intentionally unfurnished sort of way. Everything was silvery gray, even the floor.

"Come into the kitchen," Gilbert said. "I'll make cocoa."

I followed him and watched as he put milk into a saucepan. There was a bulletin board with photos of a younger-looking Gilbert with two little girls.

"Are these your kids?" I asked. For some reason, it hadn't occurred to me that Gilbert might be a dad.

"Yes," he answered briefly.

"Where are they now?"

"They're grown-up. Emmy," he pointed to one of the photos, "lives in Scotland and Sarah is in school in California."

"Where's their mom?" I asked.

"Divorced."

"Oh," I said. "Then you live here by yourself?"

Gilbert measured cocoa into the saucepan. "Yes. What's your good news?"

I felt suddenly shy. "Did you know there's a really big problem with companies using child slave labor for cocoa production in the Ivory Coast?" I asked.

Gilbert stirred slowly but didn't reply.

"I found myself a violin teacher," I admitted. "She's at Juilliard and I think she's going to be so great. I met her the same day I met you, when I auditioned, so I guess that turned out to be the single-most karmic day of my existence."

"How'd you find her?" Gilbert handed me a steaming mug.

I explained.

Gilbert sighed and sat down at the table. I sat across from him.

"Annie, we really were working on finding you a teacher."

Yeah, but I suspected that they were working the way I was currently working on my trig homework. Not really.

"I know," I said aloud.

Gilbert smiled at me. "I hired you partly because of your Berry-like habit of rushing into doing what you thought was best. But sometimes I wish you weren't quite so much like the character."

"Gilbert, I'm not Berry," I said. In this week's episode, Berry had become a social pariah because she had turned in the kids who were blackmailing Hallie Masterson's character to the head-master. I doubted I would ever have that much nerve. "I'm *me*," I said loudly.

Gilbert just raised his eyebrows.

chapter 18

Because I am the champion queen of snooze-button slapping, I was unsurprisingly late for Monday's 7:00 A.M. call. By the time I raced into the makeup trailer, the rest of the cast was already there and halfway coated in their requisite orange face cream. Grumpily I flung myself in front of Max, who raised his eyebrows at me.

"Well, it doesn't look like the cat dragged in anything very stylish *this* morning," he said, whisking a smock around my shoulders.

I moaned slightly. "Is there a cappuccino around?" The nice thing about being an actress is that it's almost expected that I will flounce around with great commotion about things like coffee. "I need a cappuccino," I repeated dramatically. Of course, I had only started drinking coffee the previous week since the chances of me being alert enough to utter memorized lines at quarter past dawn every morning were, well, nonexistent. I really thought I had a viable case for age bias; everyone knows teenagers need more sleep than other people and—as the only authentic teenager in the cast—I should obviously be allowed to come in at some point after the sun had *definitively* risen.

Max began a painful procedure that he calls exfoliating and I call Brillo-padding my face. "Annie, I hate to be the bearer of bad news, but isn't it a little late for coffee?" he asked. "You're due on-set in less than twenty minutes."

I winced. This would be the third time that I was going to delay filming out of my own sheer and inexcusable laziness. Shoot shoot shoot. "Can you get me done in time?" I pleaded to

Max. "I don't want to make everyone else wait around for me again. Please."

"Probably." Max began the moisturizing process. "But maybe you ought to think about taking Gilbert up on that wake-up call offer."

I nodded.

"*And,*" Max added, "I don't want to hear any complaints if you look like the Grim Reaper in your scenes. You know that you always look best when we have the full time to get your face in shape."

I opened my mouth to retort, but before I could get out even a *Maaaax,* the door to the makeup trailer swung open. Gilbert stalked in, accompanied by a plastic bombshell. It's not like I was trying to notice this or anything—but even from across the room, I could see her boobs were ginormous. Like, pretty much the size of my head.

"Hi, everyone," Gilbert said loudly. "Starting this afternoon, there's going to be some script changes. We're bringing in a fabulous new character, played by the fabulous Robin Field." He gestured to the bombshell. "So, with apologies for the delay, I'd like you to take the morning to get the changes down and get to know Robin and we'll begin filming at one." He passed around a stack of new scripts. I took one and sneaked a puzzled glance at Crane and Hallie. They looked as confused as I did.

As soon as Gilbert left the room, Max smirked at me. "Looks like some sleepy girl was saved from making everyone else late yet again."

"I didn't know we were getting a new cast member," I said unenthusiastically. Frankly, I liked the cast exactly the way it was. And Robin Field didn't exactly look like a kindred spirit.

"Go meet her. My hunch is there's a bit more to the story than Gilbert let on." Max pushed me gently off the makeup chair without even bothering to remove the orange foundation which now covered approximately a third of my face. I could actually feel a stiff dividing line where the makeup ended and my skin began.

I walked over to where Hallie and Crane and Frank were greeting Robin, who appeared to have applied a full face of makeup before coming to the studio. This made me feel a bit old girl; after all, I had gotten over that little vanity by the third day of filming.

"Hi," I said, sticking out my hand. "I'm Annie." Up close, Robin was almost too perfectly formed. Except for the small freckle on the side of her neck, I would have thought she was a cyborg.

She glanced at me coolly. "I know."

"So who's your character?"

"I transfer to Country Day after getting kicked out of prep school."

That sounded much more interesting than dweeby Berry.

"You'll probably be archrivals with me then," Hallie laughed.

Robin surveyed her. "Maybe. I don't know what they'll have me do." She paused. "Except for be the troublemaker."

"How'd you get the audition so late?" Crane asked. I could see Frank flinch.

"Oh, I didn't audition," Robin said, her MAC-glossed lips uttering each word with precision. "Daddy got me the dailies from the first episode, and the instant I started watching I just knew it was going to be a hit. So I told Daddy that I absolutely had to be on the show. He didn't really want me to, but let's face it." She shook her artfully dyed blond hair. "We were always just waiting for the right vehicle for my acting career."

"You're Richard Field's kid," Crane said flatly. I could see Frank flinching again, as though somehow he could prevent Crane from talking.

"Yes." Robin simpered.

Crane shook his head slowly. "Welcome aboard." He leaned over and pecked Robin on the cheek.

"Yes, welcome." Hallie did the same, so I followed her lead. When I air-kissed Robin, I caught a whiff of some undoubtedly expensive but extremely powerful perfume.

"Who's Richard Field?" I asked Crane a few minutes later, as we headed off to learn our new lines.

He rolled his eyes at me. "Come on, Annie. CEO of Spider Broadcasting? Man whose name is rubber-stamped across the bottom of all your paychecks?"

"Oh." I was quiet for a second. "So she just said she wanted to be on the show and now she is??"

Crane nodded.

I tried to absorb this and failed. "Well, I really don't feel like memorizing a whole bunch of new lines just for that," I said.

Crane laughed. "When do you?"

"But," I continued as though he hadn't said anything, "at least now I get to have a cappuccino."

Once again, good karma had saved Annie Hoffman from humiliation and despair.

Excerpt from *Variety,* September 15:

Debuting tonight, with a catty, cooler-than-thou cast, Spider Broadcasting's *Country Day* splashes into a season of otherwise sluggish programming. The series premiere introduces us to the love quadrangle of teen temptress KIT WINTERS (the exquisite Hallie Masterson), her ex-boyfriend/current nemesis SNIDER GREEN (Carter Corbin), latest conquest JODY HOLT (Crane Renfrew), and Jody's infatuated neighbor, BERRY CALVIN (Annie Hoffman, the only cast member who's actually set foot in a high school in recent memory). Despite inconsistent acting and a melodramatic script, we predict only the highest of Nielsens for this gripping prime-time soap.

chapter 19

I realize that there are some very important differences between the North and South (i.e., a war was waged), but lack of air-conditioning pretty much tops the list, as far as I'm concerned. The temperature had hovered in the low nineties for over a week. This meant that there were actually "urban heat alerts" on the weather every morning. Earth to New York: If there were AC everywhere rather than only every seven places, people would not be in such imminent danger of heatstroke and you wouldn't have to scare everyone silly. Seriously, it's like they expect the whole city to drop flat if they don't get eight glasses of water.

At any rate, I had been home for exactly ten minutes when I realized that Aunt Alexandra's tiny window unit wheezed noisily but did not actually produce cold air. Jason was due pretty much immediately for tutoring. I called him.

"We can't work here. Aunt Alexandra only has one window air conditioner and it's circa 1958. I'm melting."

Jason laughed. "You have another place in mind?"

"The Arctic Circle?"

"Right. Well, would the Starbucks on the corner work instead? Last time I was there, I got frostbite just waiting for my latte."

"Absolutely. See you there."

A funny thing happened on the way to Starbucks. I was just turning onto Broadway when a guy jumped in front of me and began clicking away. Instinctively I threw a hand up against my face. This was mostly to hide the fact that I looked like a half-dissolving refugee from the House of Wax.

"Annie, where are you going?" the guy called.

I stopped. "Starbucks."

"Are you a Starbucks fan?"

"Well, sure. They have air-conditioning."

The guy lifted his camera again and began clicking away.

"Please, I look gross," I begged.

Click. Click.

This was weird. And bad. And, frankly, very creepy.

"Why do you want pictures of me?" I asked.

"That's for me to know and you to find out."

"I don't understand. And I seriously look gross right now."

The guy shrugged. "Doesn't matter to me. Or, I bet, to a lot of people."

"Well, I'm going to go now. I'm going to be late," I said, for lack of a better option. "Nice, um, talking to you."

Clicks followed me as I walked down the rest of the street. Weird. *Weird.*

Jason was waiting for me when I got to Starbucks, reading *Spin* and sipping an iced coffee. He was sitting in one of those big purple armchairs they have. I flung myself down in the armchair next to him.

"The craziest thing just happened," I said. "I was walking over and this guy just started taking pictures of me."

Jason drank some coffee. "Congratulations," he said dryly. "Your very first paparazzi."

"Oh, he wasn't papa . . . ," I began, then stopped. "Oh," I said stupidly. "What do you think he's going to do with those pictures?" I asked. It was kind of silly, but it had never really occurred to me that the show I spent so much time filming might actually make it onto television, where people would *watch* me.

"Sell them."

"But why? I can't imagine anyone would want to buy them. It's just me, not like me and Hallie or other famous people that are actually worth caring about. I mean, I'm frankly not all that cool."

"Well, I know that," Jason said. I wrinkled my nose at him. "But you're on a series that's about to hit the big time. And that makes you important and those pics worth some money."

"People are going to be drooling over Hallie and Crane!" I protested. "Not me."

"It's going to be a hit show. My uncle says everyone at the network is talking about it."

I grinned. "Really?" So my lovely little bubble of prepremiere filming was gone. Big deal. That's what bubbles do. They pop. It's practically the reason for their existence.

Jason nodded. "You're lucky."

"Well, obviously." I kicked my legs happily over the side of the armchair. "Think about it. Up until now, I've had the most boring life known to mankind. Honestly. And then suddenly I'm plucked from oblivion." I stopped, not sure how to say what I felt. "I've just always been really boring. OK, not boring, maybe. Just average." I shrugged and looked at Jason. "It's nice to be un- usual for a change."

Jason leaned forward so that his shaggy bangs almost covered one eye. "I do think you were lucky before all this."

Oh, right.

"I would have loved your life before *Country Day*," he con- tinued.

I blinked. Jason was clearly entering sensitive-sharing mode, but I wasn't sure what he was talking about.

"I've done special, Annie, and it's not all that great," he said.

I tried to get into the Annie-as-Oprah role but found myself a bit distracted by the small dimple that appeared slightly south- west of Jason's lips as he talked.

"Since I was seven, I've been like an IQ lab rat. I skipped five grades, started college at fourteen, and grad school three years later. It doesn't help that I'm an only child." He paused. "There's such a thing as being too special, Annie, and I've been it my whole life. I would have loved to be boring—friends my own age, parents who yelled at me, an obnoxious little brother, a locker at a high school. Instead, I'm nineteen and I'm just now figuring out how to be normal. Trust me, Annie." He paused, emphatically, like Hallie does when she's about to deliver a humdinger of a line. "I would have given anything to have had that."

I was quiet for a second, thinking.

"I'm your tutor; I'm not here to sermonize," Jason said. "But I hope that *Country Day* doesn't take away quite all of the normal in you."

I fingered the ripped spine on Jason's copy of the *Aeneid*. "I do miss my friends," I admitted. "The people at *Country Day* are awesome, but they're all old and sort of jaded. Like I said I wanted to see the Statue of Liberty and they all laughed." Robin, especially. It had just been *too adorable of me*.

"Have you ever seen it?"

"Just from the airplane."

Jason stacked up his books and stood up. "Well, come on, let's go."

"Now?"

Jason grinned. "Call it a geography lesson."

chapter 20

There were drawbacks to the working life. Because of the *Country Day* schedule, Jason and I didn't start tutoring until late afternoon. This meant that by the time we got down to the ferry port we had missed the last boat. Jason was not fazed.

"This way," he announced, tearing across Battery Park.

"But the ferry port is closed." For some reason, I have a compulsive need to embarrass myself by stating the obvious.

Jason kept going. "Staten Island," he said, gesturing one arm toward the harbor. "The ferry runs twenty-four hours a day and we can get a totally gorgeous view of the statue."

The things I still didn't know about New York could probably fill a book. Maybe, given my apparent celebrity status, I could actually endorse a guidebook: *Things Annie Hoffman Didn't Know About the Big Apple.* The first chapter could be all about Juilliard.

A few minutes later, we were on the deck of the ferry, pulling into the harbor. From the way people talked about Staten Island, I thought it was far away. But you could actually see it from the deck the moment we left. It was not quite sunset. I leaned over the railing and watched the water churn below us.

"This is pretty cool," I said. Jason joined me at the railing. "So how did you get to be normal?" I asked.

"Dunno, really. I guess it became easier as I got older and everybody else's mind caught up with me and I caught more up with everyone else in chronological age."

"Do you ever miss being, like, a prodigy or whatever?"

"Rarely." We stared at the water for a while. "I'd rather tutor and teach other prodigies how to be normal."

"That's hardly what you're doing with me," I argued. "I am so definitely not a prodigy." Unless you could be a prodigy in self-humiliation, in which case I might admit to a natural flair.

Jason nudged me. "Shh. Look." He pointed and I could see the statue moving in front of us, blue and enormous and lit up for nighttime.

"Wow," I said inarticulately.

Jason smiled. "Amazing, right? I never get tired of it."

"It looks just like the photos."

"You expected otherwise?"

"Well, not exactly." The ferry had almost crawled past the statue by now. "It's fabulous. But, hmm." I paused. "It almost looks fake. I guess because I've seen so many photos, over and over, that now when I really see it, it seems fake."

Jason nodded. "Yeah, I know what you mean. That happened to me when I saw the Eiffel Tower." We were quiet for a long time.

"I've never been to France," I said at last. "Or anywhere else. I mean, I've never even been to *Canada*."

Jason made a face. "I got shipped all over as a kid. There was a group of us identified as geniuses and we made visits to all these clinics all over the world."

"That's awesome," I said admiringly. I think the most exciting trip I ever made was to Disney World with the Girl Scouts, when Sarah got sick all over me on Space Mountain. This, I admit, was not her fault, because Sarah has the motion tolerance of a trilobite ossified in stone for the past twelve millennia—but it still doesn't go down in history as an enviable travel excursion.

"Meees Hoffman," Jason said in a thick accent, "now please. You must answer these seventeen thousand personal questions."

I shrugged. Was he seriously complaining about this? "There

are worse lives than being brilliant and well traveled," I pointed out. Then, because the sun was setting and bathing Jason in a completely cinematic golden glow, I stopped being obnoxious and moved closer to him. It was still hot out, but for some reason I found myself shivering anyway.

chapter 21

Jason and I rounded out the evening by walking up to Little Italy and inhaling absolutely enormous plates of pasta. Maybe it was getting in touch with my normal, nonprodigy self, but I sailed onto the set the next morning a full twenty minutes before call. Crane was already there, scratching a wriggly cocker spaniel puppy on its belly.

"Oooh. You did it!" I bounced over. Crane had been talking about getting a dog for I-don't-even-know-how-long. "Hi, sweetheart," I cooed, kneeling beside him and rubbed the dog's long floppy ears. "Oh, he's so adorable." The dog rolled its head ecstatically against the floor. "What's his name?"

Crane grinned. "*Her* name," he emphasized, "is Molly."

"Oops." I flopped Molly's ears up and down a few times.

"You all set for this morning?" he asked.

"Sure." Today, we were filming a scene of Berry playing the violin. This had been planned for a few weeks ago, but then Robin came and it messed up the scene order, so we'd had to postpone. This would be the first time that I played in front of the cast, to say nothing of 15 million viewers. I should have been nervous, but the violin is really familiar to me and nowhere near as strange as pretending to be someone else talking to someone else who is also pretending to be someone else, if that makes any sense.

An hour later, I was dolled up to the absolute best that the hair and makeup staff could manage. Almost all the cast had gathered to watch. Even Gilbert, who pretty much never came to filming, showed up. I'd wanted to play this really haunting Chopin nocturne that I'd been working on with Helena. But The Writers—a very influential group of people I'd seen exactly once—had preferred something fast and showy. (The Writers sort of remind me of the end of *The Wizard of Oz,* when you realize the big great scary wizard is just a little bald wimp. They seem really important but are honestly just as geeky as I am, and that's why they manage to make Berry's dorkiness so terrifically authentic.) At any rate, I'd settled on this Shostakovich piece that involved turbocharged finger work and is pretty much the most wild, whirling, surprising music that I know. I sort of feel like I've jumped off a cliff when I start to play.

That morning was no exception. The adrenaline from playing in the fake *Country Day* orchestra room, underneath all the spotlights and with everyone watching, kicked in. I could feel my fingers going a bit faster than they should, so I slowed my pace. When I was done, it was totally quiet, and then one of the sound guys started clapping. Slowly, everyone else joined in. I stood there, feeling drained.

"Fantastic," breathed Dana, who was the director that week. "Now, let's do it again."

I tucked my carefully blown-out hair back behind my ears (Max would no doubt have a fit), readjusted the chin rest, and picked up my bow. By this time, I was so immersed in the music, I could have played it another twenty times without complaint. But it only took two more takes before Dana called it a wrap. By that time, some of the crowd had left. Quietly I walked back to my trailer to change from Berry's clothes back into my own. As I was fastening the buttons on my cardigan, there was a knock on the door. I opened it. Crane, Hallie, and Robin all stood there grinning.

"How do you do that?" Hallie squealed. She threw herself

down onto the couch. "I mean, honestly. If I could do that, I'd never act again."

I decided not to mention that the only reason I was acting was pretty much directly because Juilliard thought I couldn't play. "Thanks," I said instead, looking around for my shoes.

"How long have you been taking?" Hallie asked.

"Since I was six." My shoes had vanished. "Do you see my shoes anywhere?"

Crane and Hallie and Robin glanced around lazily. "They're Mary Janes," I added. "Black. Low heel." Next, I could put a picture on the back of the (soy) milk carton on the catering table. "I could have sworn I left them in the middle of the floor."

"Oh no!" Crane bolted off the couch and dove under a small table. He straightened, dangling what appeared to be approximately three-quarters of my shoe. I wasn't sure where the rest of it was. The strap was shredded and the front edge appeared equally mangled. "Annie, I am *so sorry*. I'll replace them; I promise."

I didn't get why he was so upset. "You don't have to. But where's the rest of my shoe?"

"Probably in Molly's stomach."

"Oh. Right." I fingered the ragged leather. I had kind of liked those shoes.

"She chews things," Crane added unnecessarily.

Robin slid off the couch and joined us. "Look on the bright side, Annie," she said, throwing an arm around my shoulder. "Now we can get you something a bit sexier."

I glanced at Robin's feet, which were crammed into some exceedingly pointy concoctions. When angled the right direction, the heels could probably draw blood.

"I don't know if I can walk in something like that," I said honestly.

Robin laughed a sort of tinkly laugh. "You'll learn."

———

That afternoon, as soon as we finished shooting Robin and Hallie having a drag-down fight, we went to Robin's favorite shoe store, which was in SoHo. Molly, on a leash, trotted happily beside Crane.

"You get whatever you want, Annie," Crane repeated as we pushed through the frosted glass doors. "Seriously, I'm so sorry. Molly should have never gotten into your dressing room."

I shrugged. "You're probably going to get me a much nicer pair of shoes than those were," I said. I picked up a pair of black stilettos and flipped them over. Three hundred dollars. I could feel my eyebrows raise. "Definitely a much nicer pair," I amended.

"Not those." Robin set the stilettos back on the shelf. "We want something a little more flirty."

"I fail to see how there could be anything flirtier than five-inch heels," I said.

Crane snorted. He had let Molly off her leash, and she was bobbing around the store. "Are you sure that's wise?" I asked, pointing at Molly, who was sniffing an open shoe box. "I mean, considering?"

"Robina! Darling!" A seventeen-foot-tall woman descended on our little group and proceeded to air-kiss—yes, actually air-kiss—Robin.

"We just haven't got the new Pradas in yet. You know I would have texted *immediately* if miracles had happened." The saleswoman's already gaunt cheeks caved inward with each word.

"Actually, Maxine, I'm here on a different mission." Robin flickered her perfectly lined eyes in my direction. Maxine glanced, then did a none-too-subtle double take. Maybe it was because she recognized me or maybe it was because my disastrously unchic outfit looked even worse next to her own leathered splendor.

"Crane's dog ate my shoes," I said. This was perhaps unnecessary, since I was wearing the shredded shoes, which one of the cameramen had duct-taped together for me. "He's treating me to a new pair."

Maxine's cheeks sucked even more dangerously inward. "Annie, of course." She pursed her purple lips. Then she snapped her fingers and vanished.

"How often do you come here?" I asked Robin, fiddling with the edge of a thigh-high green python boot.

"*Constantly,*" Robin drawled. "Those are awesome." She pulled the green boot off the shelf, stepped neatly out of her pointy shoes, and zippered the python around her leg. "Hmm," she mused. "I already have a pair like these."

"I wouldn't have thought that was possible," I said honestly.

Robin ignored me and pivoted on the chopstick-sized spike heel. "Annie, can I make a small comment?" she said.

"Uh," I stumbled.

"I don't think *Alabama,*" she made it sound as remote as Saturn, "is exactly a fashion mecca."

"I'm not going to argue," I said good-naturedly, watching Crane intercept Molly from licking the foot of a well-dressed woman. I wondered what it would be like to be Robin and feel completely at home in a store like this.

Robin beamed at her reflection. "Maxine, I have to have these," she announced.

"I thought you would," Maxine said, returning with a tower of boxes. To me, she ordered, "Sit."

I sat.

Maxine pulled off my shameful, taped-up Mary Jane. "You're

exactly like your character," she said, slipping a spiky, zippered number onto my foot.

"Not really," I protested automatically. Wardrobe would never let Berry walk a single step in duct-taped shoes. I stood up—for a millisecond—before dropping, wincing, into a chair.

"I can't even stand up in these," I said.

Maxine gave Robin a besieged look and wrenched the shoes from my feet.

"She'll learn," Robin repeated, exchanging her python monstrosities for the zippered shoes. Maxine slid something brown and scrunchy and suede on my foot.

"They're too dressy," I said.

Robin glanced down. "Too medieval," she decided.

The brown scrunch was replaced with hot pink patent-leather platforms.

Robin's verdict: "Too East Village."

The black loafers that I loved were "too Capitol Hill intern."

Maxine arranged my feet into some surprisingly comfortable deep purple wedges. By now, I had figured out how things worked.

"Too eggplant," I announced triumphantly.

Behind me, I heard something that might have been Crane snickering.

"*Definitely* too eggplant," Robin agreed.

Suddenly it seemed to me that the store was much more crowded than when we got there. Most of the people in the store were looking at us.

"Robin," I hissed under my breath. "People are looking at us."

Robin shoved something chocolate and crocodile in my direction. "Let them look."

I buckled the ankle straps and stood up. I could balance, which was a good sign. "Too Everglades?" I asked.

"No," Robin squealed. "Too perfect."

"How do they feel?" Crane asked.

"Well," I considered, "I wouldn't say they're comfortable. But I wouldn't necessarily say they're *un*comfortable either."

Robin grinned broadly at me. "This is an important day. Your first pair of sexy shoes."

"I have sexy shoes," I protested.

"Darling," Robin said pityingly. "Don't lie to your friends."

Were we friends? I wasn't sure. Robin made me feel more like a social charity case.

"Let me get them, Annie," Crane said. Molly was sprawled in his lap, gazing dotingly upward.

"OK." As I took off the shoes and put them in the box, I caught sight of the price. Until then, I'd been sort of caught up in TV-star fantasyland. Now I came crashing back into the hideous world of reality.

"Actually," I said slowly. "I can't let you get these."

Crane and Robin gazed at me, puzzled. "I got my old shoes on clearance at the Rack Room," I said. "These are eight hundred dollars." Just saying the numbers aloud sent a funky chill through me.

Crane rolled his eyes. "It's OK. When Robin said she'd come with us, I knew I was in for some major damage. I can afford it, Annie. I promise."

"It's not just that." I rarely get upset over major social injustices. But the cost of the shoes made me a little queasy. "I don't need shoes this expensive. There are, like, starving people and homeless people and people with dreadful diseases who can't afford doctors and it just seems weird when I already have so much."

"Annie, it's a nice idea, but you wear shoes this expensive on-set every day," Crane pointed out.

"Besides," Robin said dismissively, "no matter how starving and pitiful, it's not like anyone would really want to chow down on crocodile Manolos."

Um.

My moral conscience abandoned me.

"Um," I said aloud. "Maybe you've got a point."

chapter 22

For the first time since starting filming, I had a major secret. Now I have had plenty of secrets before, like the fact that Sarah once got sick in the bathroom at the Crimson Café and that I never even kissed anyone until I was fourteen and also that Max had to glom on about a pound of concealer when we filmed the *Country Day* pilot because I had a zit (excuse me, a *blemish*) the size of Bolivia on my chin. I am pretty good at keeping secrets. But this might have been the first time that I'd had a secret that was eventually going to become extremely public knowledge.

I was going to be in *Seventeen*.

Ew.

There was obviously nothing wrong with some people—like say anyone with the last name of Olsen—being in *Seventeen*. But to splash *me* up, in borrowed clothing, as though I were somehow a teen fashion icon, felt like a total betrayal to all my fellow violin-playing klutzes. To say nothing of the fact that I really do hate getting my picture taken and now I had to spend a perfectly good Saturday afternoon surrounded by flashbulbs. I was somewhat afraid of what people like Sharon Roberts might say about this whole affair, but I was also a good deal more afraid of what Meg or Nathan would say.

"I don't think you should think of this as a bad thing," Crane told me. "It's a chance for people to see that a violin-playing klutz can also be cool and glamorous." At my request, we'd gone to get dim sum before the shoot, because there was no way I could face *Seventeen* without an infusion of dumplings and bubble tea. Now, we were wandering, very slowly, back up-town.

I shook my head at him. "No," I corrected, examining a satin handbag from a street vendor. "That's what the old, innocent Annie would have thought. The new Annie knows that this is only going to be embarrassing and that she will somehow man-age to flub the whole thing in a way that will be described as 'charmingly naïve' in the article."

Crane rolled his eyes. "Don't take yourself so seriously, sweets. Hallie and Carter and Robin and I do articles all the time."

"You guys are pros," I whined, following Crane as he weaved expertly through the monster Canal Street crowds. While we were waiting at a crosswalk, a girl touched my arm lightly.

"My friend and I have to tell you something," she said.

"Mm-hmm?" I replied nervously. That's the kind of state-ment that tends to be followed by an announcement that your skirt is tucked into your underwear.

"We've been watching you for a couple blocks. OK, you look exactly like that girl on that new TV show, *Country Day*. Ex-actly."

"Oh," I said. "Really?" Shoot. What did people do in situa-tions like this? Fainting from nerves did not seem like either a valid or an appropriate option.

Next to me, Crane snorted. "That's because she is. Say hello to your fans, Annie."

I giggled, feeling a nervous blush seeping through me. "Sorry. You're practically the first people ever to recognize me. I don't exactly know how to act. I'm just like you guys, not a TV star or anything. Oh, and this is Crane. He plays Jody Holt."

"That's right," one of the girls realized.

"Cool!" exclaimed the other.

"Hey, Annie, can we have your autograph?"

Flattering, yes, but why on earth would anyone want my sloppy signature? What good was that? And why had they recognized me and not hunk-of-man Crane?

"Wouldn't you rather I take a picture with y'all?" I asked. "That's so much better than my awful handwriting on a smeared napkin. We can take it with my phone and then I can e-mail it to you."

The girls exchanged looks.

"You," one of them exclaimed, "are so awesome!"

"Isn't she?" Crane agreed brightly as he clicked away.

"See, Annie," he said unnecessarily as we headed uptown. "It's only you that thinks you're a dork. You've gotta get over that."

I shrugged, trying to act blasé. I could definitely get used to this whole doting-fan deal. "Isn't this the building?" I asked.

An hour later, I emerged from makeup primped to the gills. I looked like a fake version of myself, recognizable and certainly improved, but more like an Annie Hoffman action figure than flesh and blood. In fact, I looked noticeably better than I did during filming, because I was actually person-colored and not pumpkin-colored.

"This is so much fun," I gushed to Crane, as I flopped down in a chair beside him. "Look at these amazing boots." I stuck out one shiny leather-encased leg and admired its gleam. Something beneath me itched, so I shifted.

"Oh, help," the photographer said dramatically. "What on earth?"

The itching below me became a burning. I could feel my eyes, laden with sparkle shadow, begin to leak.

Crane, his face contorted in pain, jerked me out of the chair roughly.

"It's coming from beneath you," he cried. "Look."

A reddish brown stain had spread across the back of my

cream, *Seventeen*-supplied, stylish sweater. I could feel my skin throbbing. Through a haze of mascara-thickened tears, I saw the photographer run out of the room, one hand pushed across her eyes.

"It's from my purse," I realized. "Oh no."

"What?" Crane's eyes were streaming as well.

"We have to get out of here." I jerked the sweater over my head, leaving several noticeable and probably permanent makeup stains on the cashmere. My skin was still flaming, but I didn't want to take off my delicate camisole as well. Grabbing Crane's hand, I led us outside.

"What's going on, Annie?" Crane demanded, as three security guards rushed past us into the room.

"Um, Mace."

"*Mace*?" gasped one of the security guards.

"You Maced this place?" another cried.

"It was in my purse," I answered feebly. "It must have gone off by accident when I sat down. My dad gave it to me before I moved to New York"

"What, hon, to protect you against all that makeup?" the first guard asked.

"Oh, Annie," minced Crane as he pushed me into the bathroom. "You're so awesome!"

I grinned, despite my watering eyes and Mace-burning back. "You bet."

Really, a little thing like Macing a *Seventeen* shoot could happen to anyone.

chapter 23

Forget 34th Street. It was precisely ninety seconds before my violin lesson and I was in dire need of a Miracle on 63rd. Uselessly, I smeared rosin on my bow, as though that would somehow make up for a week of minimal practice. At exactly 4:00, Helena opened the door to her office, a velvet scarf tied around her thick, yarny hair.

"Oh, hi," I mumbled. "I didn't really get to practice the concerto that much this week. I mean, I wanted to. But I had to play for the show again and, um . . ." I trailed off without mentioning that I had spent three freaking hours the night before struggling through Jason's Vergil assignment. There were just so many obligations when you were America's Favorite Geek.

Helena shortened the music stand to my height. "Did you do the concerto we discussed?" She set a sheet of music before me.

"Yeah." The music looked incomprehensibly hard. "It went OK, I think."

Helena settled back down on her chair with an expression of intense concentration. "Try this."

"I'm supposed to play *that?*" I would have better luck instantaneously morphing into a watermelon.

Helena remained silent. I hoped she wasn't mad that I hadn't practiced. I mean, I'd practiced . . . I'd spent hours prepping for Berry's scene . . . but I hadn't practiced the stuff she'd given me.

"I don't think I can," I said, trying to imagine the finger work and failing. "I'd have better luck instantaneously morphing into a watermelon." Once again, I found myself wishing that my mouth didn't automatically repeat every heinous thought that entered my brain.

"You're underestimating yourself."

I *hate* it when people say that. So I tried. Really. But the bow slithered over the strings in a sequence of fading squawks and nothing I did made the timing sound right. I certainly didn't feel like the same as Berry Calvin who'd taken the *Country Day* orchestra by storm. I felt like exactly what I was: an eejit from Alabama who had absolutely no appreciation for the gazillions of fabulous chances that fate had showered upon her and therefore dared to show up unpracticed for a lesson with her incredible violin teacher.

"I'm sorry," I whispered when I was done.

Helena ignored me. "Mummph," she sighed in evident disapproval. I felt even wormier. Then she said, "We really should have taken you at Juilliard."

"Helena, that sucked," I said before I could stop myself. "I'm, like, the hugest violin failure in the entire solar system. I didn't even practice this week."

"And your playing still manages to have a more natural vibrancy than any other student I've ever had."

Gulp.

"But if you didn't master the Mozart, there's nothing else I really want to hear," she continued. "Go home, Annie. I'll see you on TV tonight."

"You watch *Country Day*?" Helena struck me as the sort of crunchmother type who might have four different looms but not a television.

"Religiously." Helena never smiles, but there seemed to be a sort of quirking up of her lips at the corners anyway. "Now go home, Annie."

I opened my mouth to ask if she meant what she'd said about my playing, but Helena cut me off.

"Good-bye."

Having been tossed out of Helena's office, I walked slowly back to Aunt Alexandra's, trying to figure out what had just happened. When I got home, the apartment was empty and I remembered that Aunt Alexandra was at her weekly canasta tournament. She gambles like a fiend and—because she is Aunt Alexandra and therefore fabulously entitled—she always wins. I threw myself on my bed, stared distastefully at tomorrow's script, and opened my cell phone to call Crane. Maybe he'd want to practice lines together.

For some reason, though, my fingers scrolled down to Jason's name.

"Annie?" he answered.

"Um, yeah, hi."

"Is everything OK?"

"I finished the translation."

"Already? You have till Thursday."

"I know." Why had I called him? We weren't exactly casual chatty, speed-dial acquaintances. "I sort of have the afternoon off from violin."

"I thought Helena was the ultimate slave driver."

"No, it's not that," I struggled to explain. "I just didn't really get to practice."

"Well, I'm hanging out in the park. Wanna bring that translation over and show me?"

Saved by the cool guy who knew what I wanted without me even having to say a word.

"OK," I said, feeling very happy. "Where are you again?"

Twenty minutes later, I was sauntering toward the Great Lawn, having changed into a skirt I'd borrowed from Berry's *Country Day* wardrobe and smeared some of Max's favorite cream blush roughly in the vicinity of where my cheekbones would be, if I had visible cheekbones. This was beginning-of-crush behavior. In the interest of necessity, I had texted Meg to keep her updated on the most important aspects of my life:

May be in luv. Jason. Uh-oh.

Needless to say, just as I walked up to Jason, my phone started the new-text-message screech.

"Oh, hey," I said to him, fumbling in my bag to muffle the sound.

"Aren't you going to get that?"

Since I was pretty sure it was Meg with some snarky comment, no. Reluctantly, I stared at my phone.

Predictable. So predictable.

"Just Meg," I said, thrusting my translation at him. He began scanning. Jason wasn't like Crane, so obviously good-looking that it caused lack of oxygen. But it was hard not to notice the way his shaggy hair crested over the top of his exceedingly long eyelashes. Yum.

Jason rolled onto his back and held the translation above him. I rolled backward beside him, being careful to cross my legs so the *Country Day* skirt didn't flash anything inappropriate. It seemed to have shrunk, magically, on the walk over.

"OK, let's take a look at this part." He pointed. "See, you've translated *domus* using the genitive. But because it's second declension, not fourth, it's actually locative."

As he droned on about the translation, I realized that my cheek was just inches from his. I had never noticed, but he had freckles also, a faint peppery sprinkle across his nose.

"Get it?" Jason finished.

"Sure," I agreed.

"That's my favorite thing about this canto," Jason said. "It's so," he paused, "delicate but *malleable*. People have translated this passage hundreds of different ways and you can still come up with your own interpretation."

"Yeah," I agreed intelligently, wondering what malleable meant.

Jason looked at me quizzically for a moment. Just when I was starting to feel really weird and scrutinized, he reached into his backpack and pulled out a copy of *Teen People*. "Maybe you've already seen this," he said, flipping it open to the back page and handing it to me.

POPULARITY CONTEST

Kit Winters may be the queen bee of New York Country Day School, but our online poll says something else. Here's how the stats stacked up on fall's hottest show:

Who's your favorite *Country Day* character?
Snider Green: 11%
Kit Winters: 21%
Jody Holt: 24 %
Berry Calvin: 44%

Turns out fans looooove Annie Hoffman's goofy good-girl character. Sixteen-year-old Ryan Rosen of Fairfax, VA, says: "Berry's my dream girl—fun and easygoing, with a great heart." And eighteen-year-old Sharla Summers from Boise writes: "I totally identify with Berry! I would never be friends with Kit or Jody, but Berry and I are one and the same." Hmmm. Maybe we should set up Sharla and Ryan?

Below, there was a big photo of me, looking shockingly terrific. I stared at the picture. It was pretty much dark out by now, so I moved away from the tree to get better light.

"Do I really look like that?" I asked, semi-aware that a mother had settled near us, with an exceedingly loud and wailing baby.

"Yeah," Jason answered.

I stared at the picture some more. "I don't think so. There's something wrong. Much as I hate to admit it, this picture's prettier than I am."

"Maybe they airbrushed it," Jason suggested.

"Probably." I looked some more. "My freckles," I realized at last. "They took away my freckles."

Jason looked at me and then back down at the picture.

"Oh, freaky," he announced.

For some reason, I felt offended. "I mean, what's *wrong* with my freckles? Are they so bad they have to get rid of them?"

"Of course not. That's just what these pictures do. Fakeify you. Your freckles are great."

I reread the article. "This is pretty amazing, though. All these people like me. I thought they'd be more into Hallie or something."

"They like Berry," Jason pointed out.

"But I'm typecast, remember?" I stared across the park at the huge fringe of buildings surrounding the perimeter.

"Look, I'd better go," Jason said. "I thought you might want to see that, but I have Ultimate practice now. Unless," he shuffled back and forth, "you wanted to come."

"With you?" I asked. Squeakity squeak squeak. "To practice?"

"Sure." He shrugged. "Meet some people in New York who aren't TV stars?"

"There is such a thing?" I grinned.

Jason made a funny little squished-up face. If I were to make that face, I would look like a cross between a rodent and a Chia Pet. He just looked adorable.

"I'm not really dressed to play Frisbee." I fingered my TV-star skirt and decided not to mention the fact that team sports are the only thing in my life that have even remotely approached the horror of learning to drive. "But I'll watch."

Then I braced myself and forced in a deep breath. I had been wrong. Jason really did create that lack-of-oxygen feeling in me.

malleable: adj. From Middle English from Medieval Latin. 1) capable of being shaped or formed 2) capable of being altered or controlled. 3) adaptive; able to adjust to changing circumstances

Crush? More like an avalanche. I was living, breathing, and dreaming Jason. If necessary, I could have subsisted entirely on the richness of my fantasies. Given our Central Park bonding, I thought that maybe—*maybe*—he would want to do something over the weekend. But when it hit Friday without a single non-educational suggestion from him, I gave up. Crane was going camping in the Adirondacks that weekend and had invited me to come. I personally rate camping right up there with killer tomatoes and body snatchers in the Unbelievable Horror category. But, since a romantic intervention seemed less and less plausible, I changed into some thrift-shop Levi's and picked up a bag of marshmallows.

(Someone took a photo of me leaving the Food Emporium. News flash: Stars toast marshmallows over campfire. S'mores lovers around the world rejoice in solidarity.)

Crane—in addition to a tent, sleeping bags, and a water purifier—owned a little plot of land where he someday intended to build a cabin in his limited time away from being a lust object. It was late in the afternoon when we turned up the gravelly road to his property. I pushed my (new, Todd Oldham!) sunglasses on top of my head and stared out the window.

"Where are we?" I asked.

"A little south of Saranac Lake," Crane answered easily.

Since my knowledge of New York geography had been thus far limited to midtown Manhattan, he might as well have said "a little south of the planet Venus" and it would have given me just as much information. As Crane wound his little silver car up the mountain, the road changed from gravel to dirt. The road was now approximately the same width as the car. Thick green trees lined one side of the road. The other was bordered by an abruptly vertical cliff without a guardrail. I shut my eyes.

"It's high," I said. Hold on to your seats, folks; Annie Hoffman has once again stated the obvious.

"Isn't it great?" Crane said enthusiastically. From the backseat, Molly barked her agreement. I am not normally scared of heights, but I am also not normally *in a tiny car* when I encounter them.

"Beautiful," I answered, with my eyes squeezed shut. The car climbed higher. My ears popped.

"I might go for a hike if we get set up in time." Crane—who by now had fully morphed from Urban Teen Icon into Nature Nut—launched into a detailed evaluation of the primarily unbroken trails around his property. My eyes remained shut. The car climbed.

"My ears are popping."

"I just think it's so great to be able to be so remote." Crane ignored me. "Annie, do you realize that no one knows where we are and no one is photographing us when we walk down the street and no one can call us, 'cause there's not even cell service, and there's just," he sighed happily, "*nothing.*"

Hell, I thought distinctly. *This is hell.*

"It's pretty much heaven," Crane finished ironically.

I sneaked a peek through my lashes. Sky. Lots of it. We had to be close to the summit of the mountain. I could feel my body falling backward into the car seat. In the interest of a little theme-appropriate Camp Fire Girl distraction, I tried to envision the melody to "Kum Ba Ya" for the violin. Second finger, then third finger on A string, first finger on E string. Or was it another third on A? Something wasn't right.

"How does 'Kum Ba Ya' go again?" I asked Crane.

"What, that old song? Isn't it like *'someone's praying, Lord, kum ba ya'*?" he sang.

Right. A reminder I didn't need. For the first time in my life, I could fully understand why someone camping might also be praying.

Just when I thought we couldn't possible get any higher, Crane pulled the car into a little clearing.

"Here we go." He opened the car door and Molly flew out, barking at the top of her doggy lungs.

I stretched my legs and stared at the small, dusty clearing and thick ranks of pines. "Wow." Pause. "Remote." Then, because I didn't want to be a total snot and because I could see how thrilled Crane was with his piece of nowhere, I added, "It's so fantastic."

I sounded pretty unconvincing to my own ears, but Crane was so outrageously delusional at this point in time that he just grinned and fussed with the ropes holding the tent to the top of the car. "My favorite place on earth," he repeated.

Three hours later, I was exceedingly glad that *Country Day* was a contemporary drama. Had I ended up on some Wild West pioneer show, I would have been killed off by episode 3 for total wussydom. After I smashed my finger with a mallet, Crane staked the tent. He also chopped the wood, built the fire, and—because I sliced myself with his Swiss Army knife—made something completely delicious for dinner involving fish and veggies roasted in a paper bag. I provided moral support and managed to feed Molly some kibble without a major first-aid incident.

(This was a spate of abnormal clutziness even for me. I had forgotten to check my horoscope that morning, so maybe it was astrologically destined. Or it could be altitude sickness. Either way, I had a terrible moment when I gazed at the blood oozing from my fingertip and realized we were in a place without cell-phone coverage, paved roads, and presumably emergency room service. If I'd cut just a little bit deeper, I could have hemor-rhaged and Crane would have had to save my life with a birch bark splint.)

As Crane fed the fire from a pile of wood he'd collected, I snuggled a little deeper into my sweatshirt.

"So, in an alternate life, you'd be a Boy Scout leader," I com-mented. The fire haloed Crane's already fair hair until it glowed. I watched as he stuck a marshmallow on a stick and resettled just outside the circle of stones he'd placed around the flames.

"Oh, maybe. But I wasn't ever in Scouts. My dad and uncle just took us camping all the time when I was a kid. We had this huge ten-person tent that we'd all cram into."

I reached for a marshmallow myself. "I'm not a camper. At all. But probably you realized that."

Crane, to his credit, said nothing.

"I mostly came this weekend because I didn't have anything else to do," I admitted. "But this is kind of great." My marsh-mallow was a nice camel color. I ate the outer crust off and poked it back over the fire so it could puff up again. I like to eat marshmallows in layers; my all-time toasting record is five layers.

"Thanks for asking me to come," I added. Then, before I could realize what total after-school-special syrup was going to ooze out of my weary city-slicker lips, I added, "I feel like you're really my friend and you like me just as I am." *Even,* I amended in my head, *if I am sort of a dork and get a kick out of being photographed by paparazzi and don't use color shampoo or special night wash or wear sexy shoes.*

"I feel the same way," Crane admitted. I gazed at him admir-ingly; he was so sensitive and warm, just head and shoulders above the male population of Bryant High when it came to be-ing in touch with his emotions. "I don't usually ask other actors to come out here with me. For me, coming here is a chance to get away from all that."

"Do you like it at all?" I asked curiously.

Crane decided his extremely burnt marshmallow was done and popped it in his mouth.

"Yeah," he said thickly through the mouthful of marshmallow. "I do." He swallowed. "See, you just fell into this by accident and Hallie's a serious theater person waiting for her chance to do something important. But I've wanted to do TV for pretty much ever. And," he reached for his canteen, "people have always told me that's what I should do. So, in a sense, I'm really lucky."

He tossed me the bag of marshmallows. I stuck a fresh one onto my stick.

"On the other hand," Crane continued, "I find it very hard to be a gay man playing a straight high school student and having a lot of teen girls writing me letters and putting up photos of me in their bedrooms and lockers and everything."

"You're gay?" I asked. Wow. Out-to-Lunch Hoffman had totally missed that. On one hand, it didn't bother me. I mean, I don't think it's morally wrong or gay people go to hell or anything like that. And even though looking at Crane caused that whole unoxygenated feeling, I didn't really think we were destined to walk into a sunset together (especially since I couldn't seem to stop lusting after my completely unavailable tutor). But something about it made me feel weird anyway—maybe because I hated that I was once again so outrageously clueless about the most basic aspects of life.

"I didn't realize," I said. Quickly I added, "I totally don't care except I'm sorry you find it hard." I tried to remember if I'd ever flirted with Crane or acted like any of the silly *Country Day* fans who had crushes on him. Although I couldn't remember any specific instances, I wouldn't put it past myself.

"It's why I wasn't drinking at Hallie's party," Crane offered. He poked the fire with a stick. "In my personal life, I'm not in the closet—but I feel I have to be more careful in public. It's not like I'm lying or denying anything, but I'd like to feel a little more in control until I figure out how people are going to react."

I moved so I was sitting closer to him. "Do you think there would be bad reactions?" I asked.

He nodded. "Some, I'm sure."

"I'm sorry," I said again. Crane patted my knee. "Thanks for telling me, though," I added.

We sat like that for a little while, just watching the fire cast sparks out of Crane's carefully arranged circle of stones. "Do you have a boyfriend?" I asked at last.

"There's someone I've been seeing, but we're not really at the boyfriend state yet." He paused. "Do you have a boyfriend?"

"Oohh," I faltered. "I've got the most massive crush." I looked up at him. "So as long as we're having a slumber party, can we pretty please talk about boys?"

Crane laughed. I took this as a "yes" and launched into a not-very-abbreviated summary of my "relationship" with Jason, beginning with the (still pretty mortifying) hair-washing incident. I'm sure that being able to tell a story concisely is a skill worth cultivating, but I have to say that I find it really difficult to leave out the nonessential details for the simple reason that everything seems important to me.

When I was finally done, Crane said, "So here's what I think." He poked the fire a bit. "The guy obviously likes you."

It was pitch-black dark, but somewhere in the world the sun was shining.

"But he's probably got reservations about making a move because he's your tutor and because his uncle works for Spider and because you're becoming this hugely popular star and he doesn't want it to seem like he's into you for the fame thing." Crane paused. "You know I'm right; that *Seventeen* article just drooled over you. So you need to find a way to see Jason somehow when you're not tutoring again and you can be yourself. Like another Staten Island Ferry thing."

"We could hit the Empire State next," I offered, only half-kidding.

"You need something fun and completely noneducational," Crane mused. Then he looked at me and added, "Something where you don't get marshmallow in your hair."

TV stars are so appearance oriented. I felt sure that someone with Jason's incisive intelligence would be sure to overlook such transient and petty physical lapses.

chapter 25

When I walked into makeup on Monday morning, the first thing I heard was a champagne cork popping.

"Champagne," I told Robin, who was frothing the bottle into plastic cups. "Not just for breakfast anymore."

Hallie grabbed a glass and tossed some back. "Didn't you hear? We hit number one last week." Her voice took on a higher, more excited pitch. "Annie, we have the highest Nielsens of any debut show this season! Spider's thrilled, obviously. There's going to be a huge party to celebrate, something absolutely enormous."

Max walked in and immediately slapped a steaming wash-cloth onto my face. I gagged inadvertently. Obviously it is nice having someone else fret about my problematic pores, but I was on the verge of second-degree burns.

"Mpmmmph," I protested. Max removed the washcloth and hovered over me, scrutinizing my skin with a fervent intensity. "No champagne for the girl next door," he announced as he threw the rag over my face again.

I hadn't known I wanted a glass until he said that.

"OK," I said as Max removed the towel. He handed me an expertly frothed cappuccino that had been delivered from the canteen. Gratefully I took a sip as Max pulled out the Brillo pad. Pain. Also not just for breakfast anymore. "That's skin, you know, Max. It doesn't regenerate automatically."

"Don't be a baby."

I bit my lip. "Is this party going to be a megadeal?" I asked him quietly.

"I imagine so. Red carpet and everything."

I thought for a second. Maybe this was *it:* the celestial star alignment destined to catapult me into romantic bliss with Jason forever and ever. I would ask Jason to the party. Really, it made perfect sense. I was new to the city, didn't know many people, and it would be utterly mortifying for a TV star of my growing celebnitude to show up *alone*. There was no way he could refuse. I envisioned myself in a fabulous, sophisticated dress, sort of like the one Hallie had worn on-set last week. The minute he saw me, Jason would decide that it was obviously pointless to deny his feelings and we'd dash off to the party in a haze of kisses. I mean, this Romeo and Juliet garbage was for the birds. No one was going to end up, like, dead in a tomb if we went out.

"Will you, um, will you?" I said aloud to Max.

"Spit it out."

"Well, I'll need a fabulous outfit, right?"

"Your prom dress won't cut it for this party?" Max asked.

"It's from the Youth Orchestra Ball, thank you very much." I sighed. "But yeah." I swiveled around in my seat. "Max, come on, please go shopping with me. Please," I begged.

I was groveling. Max tilted my chin upward and squinted at my forehead.

"Another blemish? Honestly, Annie, are you using that night wash like I told you?"

"Max, you didn't answer my question," I pleaded.

"Like you ever answer mine," he groused. " 'Oh, Max, of course I use your night wash,' " he squeaked in a falsetto. " 'That's why I have pimples the size of the Ritz.' "

"Max!" Shouldn't 10 million viewers give me an exemption from facial surveillance?

"All right." He dabbed alcohol on my T-zone. "Stop your whining. I'll take you shopping. But you're barking up the wrong tree. You should be asking *Country Day*'s other little miss to help on this mission."

"Other little miss?"

Max brandished the Brillo pad again. I felt myself shrinking in the chair. "Other little miss?" I repeated.

"Blond Barbie with famous daddy? Heard of her?"

I glanced quickly around, but Robin was guzzling champagne and flipping through *W* and seemed oblivious.

"Robin?"

"Yeaaahh." Max drew the word out so it had at least four syllables.

I stole another panicked look around. "Max, I can't go shopping with her. I'm too scared."

"Look, doll, I'll help you. But if you want something that'll land you on the best-dressed list, I'd play friends. Trust me: *Entertainment Weekly* says there's no other teen with style like Robbie."

Something Max said clicked. "Teen? How old is she? I thought she was Hallie's age or something."

"Sixteen, darling, same as you."

I could feel my jaw literally hanging. I struggled to close it. Unfortunately, shutting my mouth has always been an unexpectedly difficult task and the present moment was no exception.

"She's my age??" I tried to whisper this, but somehow the words came out superloud. "I mean," I repeated, "*my* age?"

"Darling, her sweet sixteen was a few months ago and her daddy practically had to go into therapy just to get through it. Or so the Spider Mill claims."

I absorbed this. I'd heard Robin mention school before, but I assumed this was somewhere in her distant past. She certainly was not currently embroiled in fifteen hours a week of precollege prep.

"She looks so old. And so perfect."

"I think a lot of the perfection is recently acquired." Max smirked.

"Seriously?" I asked.

Max nodded sagely. I giggled despite myself. "Everywhere?" I asked, glancing down significantly. He winked. I giggled again.

"She just looks and acts so much older than me," I mused. I mean, why did time practically stop if a glass of champagne even entered my field of vision, but Robin could clink flutes with the whole cast? It wasn't a double standard, more like a quadruple one.

"You think she'll get me a fabulous outfit?"

Max nodded.

I considered. "Like much more fabulous than anything you could concoct?"

Max nodded again. "Regrettably," he answered.

"Then I guess it's time to make friends."

chapter 26

I'd gotten a hint of what it was like to go shopping with Robin with the shoe episode. But now that we were smack in the enormous private dressing room in Takashimaya—which is this pretty fabulous Japanese department store on Fifth Avenue—I was beginning to have a total Goldilocks complex. It was like I'd snuck into the couture equivalent of the Three Bears' house and was now trying to force my way into the clothing version of too hot porridge: i.e., a flame-colored, extremely skimpy dress.

"I love it," Robin said admiringly. She was perched on a fluffy stool that had no business in the Three Bears' house but could easily have subbed for Miss Muffet's tuffet.

"It's not too, um, hot?" I asked. "Or too little?"

"Please," Robin said. She flung open the dressing room door and Gigi, the saleswoman who'd been assigned to cater to our every need, came in.

"Very lovely," Gigi said approvingly. She reached out and fingered the cloth around my ribs. "We'll just take this in," she said.

"I think it fits fine," I said.

"And lift the straps and maybe shorten this," she continued as though I hadn't said anything. Then, *without any warning,* she stuck her hand down into the wrapped V which stretched across my chest.

"Mmph," I gasped in surprise.

"And we'll obviously add a little padding to the bosom," she finished casually.

"Oh, don't worry about extra padding," I said.

At the exact same moment, Robin announced, "She needs all the help she can get."

"OK, *no*," I retorted, stripping the dress off. "Can we find something else?"

"Fine." Robin tossed up her hands. "Try this." She flung a long silver dress in my direction. Obediently I slipped into it. A good five inches of satin puddled around my ankles. Gigi lifted the hem up and she and Robin began circling me.

"No," Robin said at last.

"Definitely no," Gigi agreed. She handed me a puff of something white and sparkly. "Try this."

"Is this a tutu?" I asked.

"Volume is in this season," Robin answered, opening a bottle of Pellegrino from the tea cart that had been wheeled into the corner of the room.

I turned to face her. "Not this much volume."

She made a face. "You may have a point."

There was also something wrong with the too cutesy lavender number and the severe red sheath and the exceedingly orange taffeta monstrosity.

"I thought orange would go with your coloring," Gigi said disappointedly. I could have clued her in on that one really quickly had she and Robin actually listened to any of my feeble whimpers. I wondered if Max's endorsement of Robin's fashion taste was actually some kind of horrible practical joke, a completely obnoxious way to get back at me for my sporadic use of his special pore-refining face wash.

"We've got to be missing something," Robin said. She flounced out of the dressing room and returned a moment later with another armful of hangers.

"I have a good feeling about this one," she said, handing me something black.

By now, I had a thoroughly exhausted feeling, like I'd spent a sleepless night in Mama Bear's too squishy bed. I put the dress on anyway. It was a halter, short, with a kind of flowy skirt and an extra black ribbon that wrapped around under my chest and tied.

"Actually," I said slowly, scrutinizing myself in the mirror, "this one is just right."

"Just right?" Robin demanded. "It's a triumph."

I grinned. "Yeah, OK, it's perfect. I like it because it's so modern, but at the same time the flowy wrap part is almost Grecian."

Robin began tweaking the ribbon so it draped more to the side of the dress. "I don't get it," she said. "You look normal and even cute sometimes. But you open your mouth and it's like attack of the nerds."

Three weeks ago, a comment like that would have crushed me. Today, I merely turned and swished my skirt in satisfaction. Gigi checked the label of the dress and flipped open her cell phone.

"Jean-Claude? C'est Gigi." She began chattering away in French. Supposedly, Latin is the mother tongue and makes it easy to understand all other Romance languages, because they're all derived from it. I think this is some big lie that Latin teachers tell you to cover up the fact that what you're learning has been totally worthless for the past two millenniums. Er, millenni*a*.

"Jean-Claude will be honored for you to accept this dress as a gift to wear at the party," she said at last, in English.

"What?" I asked.

"Thank you, Gigi, and please thank Jean-Claude as well," Robin said formally.

I gaped at Robin as Gigi left the dressing room. "Do you know how much this dress is worth?"

Robin capped the empty Pellegrino bottle and tossed it into the trash.

"Jean-Claude will sell about twenty of them once you're photographed wearing it. Annie, this party is going to be covered by *everyone,* and Jean-Claude wants you wearing his stuff. Take the dress."

My arm didn't need much twisting. It really was just right.

chapter 27

Life just kept getting better. Jason was coming to the *Country Day* party.

In the end, I really was too gutless to ask him casually, so I took the cowardly-but-witty route. In the middle of some chemistry homework, I inserted my own equations:

Annie = (needs to go to party) (Country Day) + (two
          weeks from Friday)
Party = (fabulous fun)²
You = (also invited) + (more fun) / (hope you can
          make it)

He didn't say anything about it, but when he handed me back comments he had written *party = yes* across the top of the paper. I pretty much fainted when I saw it. I mean, I had developed a whole long list of well-thought-out—but thankfully irrelevant—arguments in case he thought it was somehow inappropriate. If I'd known it was this easy to ask a guy out, I would have seriously done it forever ago.

At any rate, the party was on a Friday and we got the afternoon off from filming to prepare. In my case, preparing meant I was lying around Aunt Alexandra's boudoir room reading horoscopes and waiting for Max to come and style me for the party. Aunt Alexandra decided the occasion merited a celebratory gimlet. Except—horror of horrors—we were out of limes.

"That," she announced, drawing her pointy nose even higher in the air than normal, "is simply unacceptable."

(Sometimes I think Aunt Alexandra would be a better TV star than I am. If I were to walk around saying, *That is unacceptable,* I would sound like a preschool teacher. She just sounded like Planet Earth was falling down on the completely appropriate job of making her life as easy as possible.)

"There's a bottle of lime juice in the cupboard," I offered. "I'm pretty sure."

Aunt Alexandra let out a ferocious sniff.

"Even more unacceptable." She scowled.

"Would you like me to get some limes?" I asked. This was a completely self-interested offer on my part. Spending ten minutes getting limes would be a delight compared to spending the next three hours with a pouting septuagenarian.

Aunt Alexandra's entire manner changed. Her Shanghai Red lips exploded into a big smile. "Darlingest," she cried. "That would be lovely."

Which is why, five minutes later, I was standing in the Express Only line at Fairway with enough limes to protect the entire British navy from scurvy.

"That's a lot of limes," said the girl in line behind me, who was about my age.

"I'm protecting the British navy from scurvy," I said automatically. "That's a lot of items for an express checkout," I added, looking at her overflowing basket.

She shrugged. "I like to live on the wild side."

I giggled. It was probably just the all-black, semi-Goth clothing, but she reminded me a little of Meg.

"You do, too, apparently," she said. "Aren't you worried I'll tell the papers about this?"

"This? What's to tell? That I'm enabling my great-aunt's fresh-lime habit?"

The girl shrugged again. "They would care," she said, pointing. I followed her finger and promptly stopped breathing.

"Holy crap," I said. "That's me."

We were up to the checkout counter by now.

"It sure is," the checkout guy said.

"Most definitely," added the girl.

I was still having trouble understanding. "That's me on the cover of *People*," I said, just to make it clear.

The girl and the checkout guy nodded, as though this were a perfectly normal event. I wasn't the main part of the cover, which was this woman who had murdered her boyfriend. But at the top corner there was a photo of me (freckled) and a hot pink caption. *Annie Around Town*. Wordlessly I reached for the magazine and found the story.

"Oh my God," I said, not sure whether to be horrified or delighted. "Where did these come from?" There was a two-page spread of me . . . *me* . . . doing, frankly, not much of anything. Apparently, this counted as news because I was *America's Sweetheart on Her Time Off*. There was the photo I'd known had been taken, when I was walking to meet Jason at Starbucks, and also the one of me with the bag of marshmallows. But there were a lot of others, including one of me and Robin shopping and me talking on my cell phone and me going into Barnes & Noble. I remembered the Barnes & Noble trip well because I'd left my Latin dictionary in my trailer and needed a new one to finish my homework. It was very weird to think that someone had been following me that whole time.

"I can't believe there are people in this world who really care what flavor Tasti D•Lite I like," I said aloud.

The checkout guy began counting my limes. "People care about pretty much everything when it comes to celebrities."

I stopped. That was sort of silly. I mean, I know people know who I am because of the show, but it was a bit much to call me

a celebrity. That distinction is reserved for someone like An-
gelina Jolie, someone with an interesting life and superhuman
level of attractiveness who doesn't spill cappuccino on her sweatshirt or get yelled at for having a perfectly normal amount of
adolescent blemishes.

I pushed the magazine toward the cashier. "I think I should
buy a copy. I've never been on a magazine cover before."

"Better get used to it," he said, swiping the magazine through.
"I think they've got a permanent tail on you."

"You think someone is photographing me *now*?" I asked,
whirling my head around suspiciously. I was wearing a University of Alabama shirt and a ponytail and was pretty sure I
looked like I'd recently emerged from the crypt.

Before I could help myself, a very familiar phrase came out of
my mouth. "Well," I sputtered. "That is *unacceptable*."

chapter 28

If Jason = Prince Charming, then Annie = Cinderella + Snow White + Sleeping Beauty + that divorced American woman who was swooped up by the King of England in nineteen thirty-whatever. Then again, that would make Robin my fairy god-mother. So much for equations. Real-life chemistry—the crackly-explosive-interpersonal stuff—was infinitely better.

Despite Robin and Hallie's hopes for some supercool club, the party was going to be at Top of the Rock, which is (just like it sounds) the top floor of a building in Rockefeller Center. I was too nervous to hang around by myself upstairs waiting for Jason, so I walked down to the lobby and fake-flirted with Jules for a bit until the car got there. When Jason stepped out of the limo to come get me, I pretty much keeled over with excitement.

I could have said something about how awesome the party would be or maybe even an insightful comment about the state of world affairs. Instead, I said, "This limo is kind of big." That was unfortunate. Jason was a (very good-looking) genius, which meant that he would hardly be into a dipwit with an uncontrollable penchant for stating the obvious. The only thing I could hope was that there was some neurological reason for this problem, like kind of a tic, and I could take a pill to get rid of it and instantly become a more scintillating human.

"Is there going to be a lot of press there?" Jason asked.

"Yeah," I answered. "According to Robin and Gilbert and everyone." I turned to look at him. "Do you think they're going to take our picture? Because I really hate having my picture taken." I was feeling a little weird. I mean, it was *stupid*. I'd been looking forward to this night for freaking ever and now I just kind of wanted to be back safely at Aunt Alexandra's. "I hate people looking at me."

"Ten million people watch you every week."

"Stop it. I'm nervous," I said before I could censor myself.

Jason smiled. "My own trick for being nervous is to start translating whatever conversation I'm having into Ancient Greek in my head." He shrugged. "You could do it for Latin."

That was so astoundingly dorky that I just started laughing. "It's a shame that whole fall of Rome thing happened and you can't get a job as a simultaneous interpreter at the Coliseum."

Jason gave me a total "shut up, Annie" look, just like Meg or Nathan would, which made me feel normal and unnervous. But when we got to Rockefeller Center, there were a lot of people waiting outside and the creepy feeling returned. Our driver couldn't even get us all the way to the door because the street was blocked off. I stared at the throngs of people. Some of them looked like photographers and some of them just looked like people, like me or Sarah or my mom or whomever.

"Wow," I said inarticulately. "This is kind of intense."

Even though the windows were tinted on our car, people were taking pictures of it.

Jason took my hand in his and squeezed it. "This is going to be great," he told me. My heart began pounding, either because of the cheering crowds or because of the physical contact. "Are you ready?"

I took another peek at the masses of people and nodded.

He squeezed the hand he was holding. "You look beautiful."

Before I could absorb this, he opened the door and gave me a gentle push onto the street. At first, I just stood there, flashbulbs popping around me, a little scared and shocked but also exhilarated. I mean, never in my wildest and most outlandish dreams had I fathomed hordes of people screaming my name.

"Annie, over here!"

I began to see blue spots from all the flashes.

"Annie, what's it like coming from Alabama to all this?"

I felt Jason step beside me and grip my hand again.

"Annie, who's the guy? Is he your boyfriend?"

"Come on," Jason said softly to me.

I smiled at him, a big happy smile sprung from genuine delight. We started walking toward the door. Then, because I didn't want to miss a chance, I turned back and beamed at the crowds. The flashbulbs popped around me, fast, almost like lightning. A guy wearing a headset weaved through the door to greet us.

"Annie Hoffman has arrived; repeat: Annie Hoffman arrived," he announced into his mike.

You better believe it.

Things were a good deal calmer and more elegant upstairs. Drop-dead gorgeous waiters—who probably had more acting experience than I did—were dressed all in white and circling the room with trays of hors d'oeuvres. In the center of the room was a big white cube of a bar. I could see Hallie leaning into the bar, laughing as she accepted a cocktail. We were really high up, seventy stories, and the view was pretty amazing.

"I love New York from a distance," I said, gesturing to the windows.

Jason accepted something on a cracker from a waiter. "I know what you mean," he answered. "It's hard for me to believe each one of those twinkly lights is a person in some way, you know, either a home or an office or whatever."

"You guys are *so serious*." Robin flung herself between us. "Mwah-mwah," she said as she air-kissed me. "You look hot." To Jason, she added provocatively, "Doesn't she?"

I've decided Robin is sort of like a puppy, just lapping up attention and excitement and doing everything she can to stir things up. I kind of envy her; I can't imagine catapulting through life so blithely and carelessly. Jason, however, looked startled.

"Jason, Robin. Robin, Jason." I pointed as I performed introductions. "Robin is the stylist responsible for my dress tonight."

"Very nice," he said. "It's kind of Grecian."

I glanced meaningfully at Robin, who rolled her eyes. "Are you clones?" she asked, then answered her own semi-rhetorical question: "You're like total clones."

A waiter interrupted us. "Lobster skewer," he murmured. Happily I helped myself. Lobster is my absolute favorite food. I mean, yes, I took biology and I know a lobster is essentially a giant cockroach. It is also, I'm sure, a morally reprehensible act to boil them alive and they probably do suffer even if they don't have advanced nervous systems. But truthfully, if forced, I could probably subsist exclusively on lobster and maybe bubble tea for at least a year.

"Do you know that they sell the McLobster at McDonald's in Maine?" Jason asked. "Totally true."

I giggled. "It used to be that eating lobster was a sign of poverty. It would be like people today eating rat or something." I grabbed a second skewer before the waiter walked off.

"Gross," Robin announced.

Just then, Karl Kasaki appeared beside us, a cocktail in each hand. It was a good thing Robin had forewarned me that he was coming as her date. As it was, Jason and I were both a little gapey. I mean, this was the first time I'd ever been within four inches of a multi-platinum-selling rock star. When it came to teen idols, I was Annie Come Lately and Karl was the real deal.

Robin took one of the drinks from Karl. "Thanks, bunny," she said casually.

"Hi," I chirped. "I'm Annie and this is Jason."

Karl angled his chin slightly downward, in what might have been a nod of acknowledgment or simply a readjustment due to swallowing a mouthful of blue drink.

"I love your music," I added. This was true. I'd listened to Karl Kasaki pretty much every day for three straight years during middle school. Karl's chin declined an additional centimeter. Meanwhile, Robin managed to down most of her cocktail in a single mysteriously delicate gulp.

"This is my *favorite* song," she squealed. Her voice was a half decibel below a full-fledged scream. "Let's dance." She grabbed Karl by the collar of his leather blazer. "Come on, join us," she called back to Jason and me.

I shrugged at Jason. "I kind of want you to meet Crane," I said. So, we wandered around and talked to Crane and then Gilbert and then to Jason's uncle for a long time. After a couple hours, it was obvious that we were pretty much the only sober people there. Even Crane was a bit red faced and tipsy.

"Don't you want a drink?" I asked Jason, who had been drinking Sprite all night. "I mean, I'm not going to, but there's no reason for you not to have something."

"I don't think anyone would care if you had anything," Jason noted. This was an understatement. Robin (whose *father* was there) had had something like seventeen blue drinks and was now sitting on top of the white cube bar with her gold sequin halter falling open enough to reveal a rather large expanse of recently acquired breast. I could have probably guzzled my weight in champagne and some responsible person with a headset would have simply scooped me into the car home. "But I don't want to drink if you don't feel comfortable," he added.

"I kind of don't want to," I admitted. "It's not the underage thing. It's just I don't really like the taste. And I've never had a *better* time because I was drinking."

Jason wrapped his arm firmly around my waist. "Well, I'm not going to have anything either. I don't think it would be very nice if you brought me to this fabulous party and then you had to spend the night taking care of your sloppy trashed date."

I leaned against him. "I dunno. That sounds pretty romantic." Slowly, as if synchronized, we walked out onto the balcony and gazed at the sparkling city spread below us. There was something very appropriate about our literally being on top of New York tonight.

"Did I tell you how beautiful you look yet?" he murmured.

"You probably better tell me again."

He smiled. We were so close that I could see a small white scar running through his eyebrow. There was a vague quivery feeling in the pit of my stomach. Gently I touched the scar.

"Where did this come from?" I asked quietly.

"Knife fight."

"Really?"

"No. Skateboard accident when I was thirteen. But it makes me look like tough."

Jason's sexiness is of the sweet variety. He looks tough the way a squirrel looks tough. Inside, I could hear the guitar intro to Karl Kasaki's "Kissing Tonight."

"How weird to be listening to a Karl Kasaski song when we're ten feet away from Karl Kasaki," I said. I wrapped my arms around Jason's neck and he put his hands on my waist.

"How weird to be Karl Kasaki listening to some random DJ play a Karl Kasaki song," Jason answered, as we slow danced (very slowly) on the balcony. If he hadn't been holding me, I might not have been able to stand up. My entire body was melting into a gooey mess. I could see Jason's eyes studying me intently.

Then, in the most wonderful weirdness of all, we were kissing, listening to Karl Kasaki sing "Kissing Tonight," with Karl Kasaki himself mingling indoors with my glamorous friends.

Tonight was the sort of night when I might accidentally leave my glass slipper behind at the ball.

ANNIE'S MYSTERY GUY!

Sweetie Pie *Annie Hoffman* stunned fans and friends alike when she spent most of *Country Day*'s exclusive party hooking up with a mystery man. Who is he? According to our sources, *Jason Halliday* is none other than Annie's private tutor, a freak-of-nature language prodigy who spent his childhood being studied by psychologists. Nepotism (surprise, surprise!) is alive and well at Spider Broadcasting; the nineteen-year-old human lab rat is also the nephew of Spider exec *Marshall Halliday*. All we have to say is that Latin's dead, Annie, and there's a whole world of far sexier guys waiting to ask you out. Jason used his uncle to get him a job and now he's using you. Don't waste your time on this loser.

chapter 29

I hadn't talked to my parents in five full days and now that we had finally connected they were, I regret to say, being total idiots.

"Annie," Dad began. "Try to look at it from our perspective. All we hear is that you went to a party. The next thing I know, I'm picking up chicken to grill for dinner and see my daughter and a strange guy making out on the cover of a supermarket tabloid above the caption 'Annie gets it on!' Not entirely your normal Thursday afternoon activity. Then, to top it all off, guess who is in line behind me? That's right, Mrs. Lyle. Who was kind enough not to mention the obvious, like the fact that I was so shocked I dropped an entire jumbo-size container of yogurt onto the floor, where it splattered on my shoes, her shoes, and most everyone else's."

Eeep. Mrs. Lyle was my elementary school principal. Her shoes tended to be black, low heeled, and very shiny; I remembered sitting, cross-legged on the floor, watching them stomp around the floor of the school auditorium. But I could think of worse people to have witnessed such a horror—like Doris the DMV person or Sharon Roberts or Kale McLaughlin, on whom I have had a crush since roughly three seconds after laying eyes on him the first day of preschool. Of course, they had probably all seen the magazine covers by now anyway. That's the funny thing about publicity: When it's something nice, everyone knows about it. And when it's *completely unjustified, horrifying, and embarrassing,* even more people know.

"So who is this man who took you out?" Dad finished.

"If you read the article, you would know."

Dad said a word that I'd never heard him say before and that is usually scribbled on the back of locker-room doors. I was very glad that I was a thousand miles away.

"He's my tutor. And it's not a big deal. He's only three years older than I am and he's great and funny and warm and you know what else? He's probably never going to talk to me ever again in my life because of this."

My blubber-to-words ratio began to get a little out of control. Now that I'd said it aloud, I realized how afraid I was that Jason would show up any minute with a tutoring resignation. I mean, not only was I young and immature and possessed only a minute percentage of his remarkable intelligence, but I was also responsible for the total public decomposition of his otherwise impeccable reputation. I had read the articles: Every single one of them accused Jason of being interested in me only because I was famous, and said I needed someone more glamorous as a boyfriend. How I had managed to con the American public into not recognizing my own inherent dorkdom was inexplicable . . . but also a relatively minor issue given the current traumatic scenario.

"Is this show too much for you?" Mom asked. "We never envisioned this kind of publicity. You shouldn't have to deal with this. Do you want to come home?"

And go back to being Annie Boring Hoffman at Boring High School? I'd rather impale myself on a spork.

"*No,*" I said as emphatically as possible through my stuffy nose.

"Well, we can't just let this happen," Mom said. "The situation is not OK."

"Unacceptable," I agreed, channeling Aunt Alexandra.

"Maybe we should come up."

"*No,*" I repeated. "Look, everything is fine. It's the same as it was last week, except the fact that my big crush is on the cover of every tabloid in America. But, please, I'm telling you that I haven't changed and I'm still normal, sane, boring Annie."

There was another long silence, but this time I didn't interrupt it.

"OK," Mom said finally. "But I want to talk to Gilbert Grayle about the situation."

I heaved a sigh of relief. Gilbert wouldn't feed me to the wolves; he needed me too much. Because people really loved Berry's character, they'd expanded my role and I was in a ton of scenes in the next couple weeks.

"I'm sure he'd be happy to talk to you," I said.

After we said good-bye, I found myself welling up again. I'd managed to convince my parents that the sky wasn't falling. Jason would be a harder sell. The only thing worse than being a closet dork was being a closet dork in need of tutoring.

How do you do your homework when your first date with your tutor was publicly condemned by the mainstream media?

How do you know if your tutor is right for you when you don't know what his zodiac sign is?

How do you know if you even still have a tutor, because you might have stupidly managed to get him fired because you couldn't possibly find a more appropriate first date than one which would be witnessed, via photographic evidence, by millions of people across America?

None of these questions were answered in this month's *Cosmo* quiz, which was more interested in whether I was aware of what kind of man I was drawn to. Frankly, I was all too aware and he was due any second. There was a pretty decent chance that by the time he arrived I might have dissolved into an anxious puddle whose contents, if chemically analyzed, would be revealed as 100 percent essential essence of idiocy.

The doorbell rang. I resisted the urge to crawl into a ball under my bed.

"Hi," I said, opening the door and staring at my toes in one singular motion.

Jason touched my hair.

"Annie," he said. For some reason, my name sounded different when he said it. I studied my bare feet industriously. Jason wrapped his arms around me. My limited self-control vanished.

"I'm such an idiot," I mumbled through what might best be described as a torrential deluge of tears. "I never imagined something like this would happen."

Jason made a small soothing noise.

"I thought the media *liked* me," I added.

"Oh, the fickle finger of fame," Jason said wryly. He led me over to the couch and we sat down, his arms still wrapped firmly around me. Now that I had started crying, it seemed absolutely impossible that I might ever stop. I would be like some cursed kid in a fairy tale, blubbering until eternity. Then again, if I *had* to be a pitiful sniveling wreck, it was nice to be consoled by the calmly long-lashed hunk of my dreams.

Here is something embarrassing about Annie Hoffman, closet geek: It would be an understatement to say that I am not very experienced when it comes to boys. The only way I could actually have less experience would be if I had been born in a sequestered French convent in the thirteenth century. I mean, I've had a sprinkling of dates and kisses and all that, but nothing ever gets off the ground. The last "boyfriend" I had was two years ago, and the culmination of our two months of grand passion was sharing popcorn at a revival of *Gone with the Wind* at the Bama Theater. Needless to say, my dear, I frankly gave a damn about my atrocious lack of experience. This meant that snuggling against Jason

was actually a kind of radical act, even though I had been re-
duced to blithering pulp.

"I never meant for this to happen," I sniffled.

"I know," Jason said, petting my hair. He was as calm as if we
had been discussing my trig homework, which—for once—
would have been a preferable topic of conversation.

"I *hate* publicity," I said vehemently.

Jason kept petting my hair. It was such a remarkably pleasant
sensation that I felt the tears stopping. I looked up, adoringly, at
him. This was probably an appropriate time for us to start kissing again.

"Deep breath," he said instead, inhaling vigorously. I imi-
tated him. "And another," he said. I took a second gulp of air.
Jason released his arms from around me. I felt suddenly cold
without them. I inched closer to him.

"Annie, the publicity is only going to get worse," he said.
"You've sparked everyone's interest and they want to know more."
He looked at me. "The media can be ruthless." He reached out a
hand to push a soggy, tear-drenched chunk of hair away from my
cheek. "I like you so much, Annie," he said. "So much," he repeated. "You have to believe me on that. But I don't think we
should be together now."

The suddenly cold feeling got combined with a suddenly
queasy feeling.

"The media's been vicious and they've seen there's as much a
market for not-nice Annie Hoffman gossip as there is for innocent Annie-gets-ice-cream gossip."

"So?" I asked.

"So, they're going to get even more vicious. Annie, our being
together is not good for you and your career. Really. You have a
chance to become someone great and this is going to blow every
opportunity you've been given."

"What career?" I demanded. "I'm just having fun with this TV thing. It's not serious for me." As I said it, I kind of knew this was a lie, because there were about seventeen hundred things I would give up if it meant I could have a fabulous life of fame and fortune.

Jason looked unhappy. "This publicity isn't good for me either, Annie. It's embarrassing," he said. I moved a microscopic amount closer to him, so that we were almost touching. "I don't want to be known for taking advantage of some famous kid," he added.

"That's totally stupid," I said. "You're *not* taking advantage of me." I stopped. More than anything, I wanted it to be five seconds ago when we were all snuggly and close. "Look, you say you like me." He nodded. I took a deep breath. "Well, I like you, too, and I think it's silly to let being afraid of publicity get in the way of that. I can handle whatever the media spits at us. Seriously."

"Annie, come on," he said. "My uncle has told me about all kinds of stuff like this before. And it's awful."

"We're not doing anything wrong," I protested. "Besides, I'm not as innocent as everyone thinks I am."

Jason raised one eyebrow, the one with the small scar.

"I just think it's silly for us not to be together. We like each other. Come on," I pleaded. I could feel the tears starting again and I blinked, furiously, to keep them from spilling. "I can handle this," I repeated. "I'm sorry if you can't."

Jason sighed. He touched my cheek again. "I do like you, Annie, but I just don't know." I stared at him, hoping my beseeching, teary look was at least somewhat alluring. "I can't be your tutor anymore. Realistically, it's not a good idea."

"Don't be my tutor then. We can find someone else." *Be my boyfriend,* I wanted to say. But I was already going overboard on the emotional groveling, so I kept quiet.

Jason stared at me for a very long time, before finally wrapping his arms around me again. I felt myself relax. "OK," he said. He kissed the top of my head.

For the first time since the party, I felt completely happy.

chapter 30

Because art imitates life, the current *Country Day* plotline involved Berry getting involved with a dishy but inappropriate male.

"Peachy," I complained to Crane. "Since the world isn't already convinced that I'm some slutty schoolgirl, this will just about clinch it."

Crane laughed. "Well, Lolita, I have to say that that school uniform can't get much shorter and tighter."

I glanced down at the tiny gray skirt and tiny heather blue sweater. "Blame wardrobe, not me." Not that I was entirely complaining. I may live in jeans and sweatshirts in real life, but given that viewership was topping 15 million, I was just as happy to be poured into well-tailored outfits that made the most of my limited curves. "I wonder when we'll start shooting," I added.

The writers had decided that Berry and Jake (the new older guy) were going to meet in Central Park at sunset, which was obviously very romantic. Weirdly, even though this all supposedly took place in Central Park, we weren't actually filming there, but in some other park up in the Bronx. The editors would splice our leafy close-ups with some footage they'd taken of Central Park a while back, so it would look like that's where we were.

At any rate, I had been sitting in a lawn chair outside for something like five hours, bored out of my mind, while Crane and Robin filmed the same three scenes over and over again.

"Kitten, you're sweaty. Let me touch you up." Max fluttered over to me brandishing a powder puff the size of Mars.

"Do we get to start soon?" I asked.

"Sunset." The powder puff descended in a cloud.

"Well, when is that?"

"Don't know, kitten; do I look like a lunar calendar to you?"

Max swaggered off. I gazed at his retreating back, trying very hard not to be irritated. I could probably have used this time to work on some of the homework that my new (really awful, slave-driving, non-Jason, unsexy) tutor had assigned, but that seemed like a good way to make myself even more miserable.

"I'm starving," I announced to Crane. This was because five hours ago I had had to go film this clip of myself reading under a tree and missed the arrival of the catering table. That kind of scene usually only takes twenty minutes or so, but there was a camera problem today—which meant that by the time we were done with filming, there were only a few crusty pieces of cheese left that had fallen off a sandwich. I suppose I could have made somebody go get me lunch, but it had seemed kind of princessy given that none of the camera crew (who also had to go lunch-less) were complaining.

"What's up?" Robin joined us. She had changed out of her fake and equally skimpy school uniform into something that was both tweedy and velvety.

"I'm starving," I repeated. "I missed lunch."

"My trainer says that we're supposed to have a six-hour gap, minimum, between meals."

"Six hours?" Crane asked. "Your trainer sounds like a freak. You'd have to have, what, the metabolism of a camel?"

"I've gone six hours," I whined. "I am perishing from malnutrition. And the sun is never, ever going to set. We're trapped in some kind of reverse eclipse where it stays in the sky forever."

Neither Crane nor Robin responded.

"The guy playing your new bf is here," Robin changed the

subject. "And I would like to note that he is extremely, extremely hot."

I perked up. "Really?"

"Settle down, jailbait," Robin said. "I want this one."

"What about Karl?" I asked, noticing that there were a bunch of people lingering around the barriers, probably hoping for a glimpse of us. There was a lot of space between the barriers and where we were, so they could probably only see the same smeary outlines of us that we could see of them. I bet they would have been surprised to know that three of *Country Day*'s famously gorgeous cast were having a boring, definitely ordinary conversation about someone else's physical splendor.

Robin rolled her eyes. "To quote someone, but I'm not sure exactly who, 'he's dead to me.'"

I giggled and started to ask what happened but got cut off.

"Annie!" Curt, who was this week's director, came over to us. He sounded distinctly annoyed. "We have to start filming before the light is gone. Come on."

I glanced up. The sky looked no more or less amber than it had a moment ago.

"Evidently it's sunset," I said, gesturing to the bright blue sky. With Crane and Robin at my heels, I made my way over to the edge of the cameras, where Max repuffed and reblushed my face and Melinda from wardrobe tweaked my clothes.

"Annie, this is Jared," Curt said. "He's playing Jake."

Hot was an understatement.

Casually, like the fabulous TV star I supposedly am, I smiled at Jared. "Hey," I greeted him.

"Hey, Annie Hoffman," he said, even more casually. We basked in our coolness for a moment. From behind Jared's head, Crane made fake goggle-eyes at me.

"OK, you guys are up. We're going to dry run it once. Annie, you start sitting right here." Curt motioned.

We ran the scene, which only took about two minutes or so. Jared was pretty good at the whole memorizing-lines thing. He didn't flub once (unlike yours truly, who managed yet again to demonstrate that she had the linguistic memory of a lesser ape). The plotline was basically that Berry meets this totally sexy older guy and lies to him to seem cooler, like saying she's eighteen and in a band. After we were done, Curt nodded.

"What I really like, Annie, is how you seem so thrilled just to be in Jared's presence," he commented.

Ah, yes, *exceptional* acting on my part.

Curt continued giving us directions and tips for a few more minutes. Then he glanced up at the sky.

"Sunset, let's go, people!" His voice carried a note of urgency. "We have to get it right the first time; otherwise the light is going to go and we're going to have to spend a ton to reshoot." He looked significantly at me. "OK?"

"Sure," I said.

The clapper clapped and we started the scene. Halfway through, I realized the light was suddenly golden. The edges of my hair lit up red instead of brown and Jared's skin looked sort of tawny. I started going into what I called Berry autopilot, when I just felt the lines coming out of my mouth exactly when they should in the way they were supposed to.

"I bet you're more exciting than you pretend to be," Jake/Jared flirted.

"Quite the reverse," Berry/Annie answered.

"I'll be calling you, Berry Calvin," he said, his eyes sort of soft and melty. He reached and touched my chin with his hand, a small stroking caress. That should have been the end of the scene. But it wasn't. Instead, Jared moved his hand around to the back of the neck. As I gaped, he drew me close and kissed me.

That was so definitely, most assuredly, *not* in the script. I could feel my heart pounding. Too stunned to respond, my tongue hung limply in his mouth. His hand moved from my neck down my back, coming to rest gently in the small of my back. As he showed no signs of letting up, I kissed back.

We kissed for so long that I was short of breath when he at last let me go. Automatically, I reached up and touched my lips. I could feel the camera angled directly at my face. When they edited, they would no doubt use an extreme close-up of my genuine shock.

"And *cut!*" Curt exclaimed. "That," he shook his head, "was absolutely brilliant."

chapter 31

Neither Robin nor I felt much like going home after the kiss that was going to launch a thousand Nielsens. So we ended up sharing a car back to Robin's favorite Village bistro, which seemed French to me but is apparently actually Belgian. I realize the distinction between the Low Countries is probably one of economic and topographic importance, but it, frankly, seemed sort of culinarily arbitrary.

"They have the most amazing fries here," Robin said, settling into her (understated chic brushed-aluminum) chair. "I can't get them because they're not on my training plan, but if you get them, then I can have some."

"I don't think your trainer knows what he's talking about. He sounds sort of sadistic." I scanned the menu. We'd had to wait for maybe five minutes before we sat down, which made me feel a lot like a real person and not like Annie Hoffman, TV Goddess. "This place is cute. Maybe I'll take my friends here this weekend."

"Your friends?"

I grinned. "So, my parents are totally worried that I'm going to get corrupted by this TV life, right?" Robin nodded. "So I convinced them that the best thing in the world would be if my two best friends could come up this weekend. I'm planning all kinds of awesome stuff. Like, I know that Meg wants to go to hang out in the East Village and I want to take them shopping, like to Takashimaya and some of those SoHo boutiques you showed me, and I want to get them tons of New York presents and go to a Broadway play."

The waiter appeared at our table. With a wink at Robin, I ordered mussels and French fries (or *frites,* as they called them here). She ordered mussels and salad and then opened the cocktail list.

"And can we have two Raspberry Riots?" she said calmly.

"I can't believe he didn't card you," I hissed after the waiter moved on. "We're practically the two most famous underage people in New York."

"If thirty is the new twenty, that makes sixteen the new twenty-one," Robin answered. The girl had an answer for everything. If I had an ounce of her general unflappability, I would probably not be such a disaster at life, the universe, and everything.

"So maybe you could come out with me and Meg and Sarah this weekend?" I grabbed the bread basket, since Robin was so clearly not going to touch that either.

"Yeah, sure, we can meet up at Angel or something." Angel is Robin's favorite club. Last week, "Page Six," which is the gossip column in the *Post,* reported that she had closed out the night by dancing on the bar. Not that I actually had the right to comment on anyone else's poor publicity, since I had apparently gone from being the girl next door to a total hussy.

The drinks arrived. Robin picked hers up right away and took an oceanic-sized swallow, but I just let mine sit in front of me.

"So, I have to ask: Was kissing Jared like the greatest thing about your day?"

I wrinkled my nose. "I think getting to eat lunch at seven at night is going to be the greatest thing about my day."

"Come on!"

"Seriously." I looked at the drink lingering in front of me. It's not like I was going to revive a chapter of the Woman's Christian Temperance Union or anything. I took a sip. I thought it would burn when I swallowed—like every other drink I'd ever tried—but it went down easily.

"I just was so not expecting it, you know." I drank some more. This was actually pretty good. "I mean, he's sexy, but it was also kind of . . ." I trailed off, not sure of what to say. "Intrusive?"

Robin giggled. "You're so cute."

"Well, it wasn't in the script!" I found myself giggling with her. "You try having surprise tongue in your mouth in front of a zillion people and then tell me it's not at least a little strange."

I giggled again. It was nice just to be with Robin and, well, relax and be normal. "You know, I used to identify with Berry a lot, but this new plotline is kind of out of my league. I would never lie to some guy about who I was."

"Why not?" Robin asked.

"Well, because, I want people to like me for who I am not because of who I pretend to be." The absurdity of the conversation struck me. "Except that's what acting is, I guess. Ten million viewers only like me because I pretend to be this other person. Is that a different situation? It's got to be. Right?"

Robin giggled again. "You're such a little thinker."

I wrinkled my nose. "Not when I'm starving. Where are my fries?"

The next morning, as I was riding to the set, I realized that last night's dinner had made it into the *Post*.

> Spotted: New BFF Robin Field and Annie Hoffman, kicking back after a long day of filming with cocktails at Mon Petit Choux.

I was dead. I was 100 percent as thoroughly dead as if I were an actual bloodless, gray-skinned cadaver donated, worthily enough, to scientific research for meticulous dissection. My parents were going to *kill* me. Yeah, we'd had the whole "we understand teens drink and while we'd rather you didn't, if you do happen to drink, we'd rather you be responsible and honest about it" talk about seventeen times. Except somehow I didn't think the sort of honesty they wanted included being written up in *national media*. Was it too much to ask that I be able to go to dinner without being tracked by the sort of infrared distance lens that was probably originally developed to detect nuclear activity in Los Alamos?

"Do you think Singapore Planet is open?" I asked Jeremiah.

"It's six forty-five A.M.," he answered.

"Yeah, but do you think they're open?"

"No."

I frowned. "I really want a bubble tea."

"We can stop on the way home."

"No," I said sulkily. "I'll be dead by then."

"Is something going on?"

"I'm awaiting death," I repeated.

"So are we all, Annie."

He may have had a point there.

"There's a small item in the *Post* that means my parents are going to kill me when they read it," I confessed.

"Mmm," Jeremiah said noncommittally.

"And it would just make everything a lot better if I had a bubble tea."

"The Singapore Planet people are asleep."

"Right," I said, sighing. I closed the privacy panel and proceeded to spend the next twelve hours writhing in excruciating mental agony.

"Still alive, I see," Jeremiah said as I got back in the car after shooting.

"Well," I answered honestly, "it's only because I'm an unusually accomplished avoider and turned my cell phone off."

Jeremiah stuck his hand through the privacy panel. He was holding a bubble tea. "You like apple, right, girl?" he asked.

"You got me bubble tea?" I squeaked.

"Turns out they open at ten."

"Thank you! This is awesome." Then I made a face "OK, I'll call my parents."

"Annie, hi!" Mom answered. "What's up?"

She sounded clueless. My heart began to beat a little more normally. They hadn't seen the item. *They hadn't seen the item.* The positive implications of this were hundredfold.

"Um, not much, just wanted to say hi," I ad-libbed casually. "And to see if you could send up my green sweatshirt with Meg and Sarah, 'cause I forgot it."

What can I say? It's much better to be lucky than good.

chapter 32

Jules said he'd be deaf for a week from the piercing screams that careened through the lobby when Meg, Sarah, and I reunited. We hadn't seen each other in two months and Sarah had a new boyfriend and Meg had dyed her hair a sort of burgundy red and chopped it into inch-long spikes and I was, well, Tabloid Superstar.

(I told Jules that Meg and Sarah weren't screaming because of me but because of his massive physical perfection. He seemed to find this hysterical, which was no doubt because his job involves interacting exclusively with emotionally taxed Upper West Siders en route to therapy, who never say hello—let alone deliver the most well-deserved of compliments.)

At any rate, no matter how earsplitting our lobby screams, we were shrieking even more thrillingly a few hours later. Jason had gotten tickets for us to hear this band at Warsaw, which is a club in Brooklyn. Meg, who enjoys indie rock in the same general way that fish enjoy gills, was in the front row waving her arms over her head. Behind her, Jason and Sarah and I screamed and danced like we were on one of those semi-lame MTV specials. It was, frankly, one of the most fabulous nights I'd had yet in the city. Jason, who was already at Prince Charming white-horse status, got elevated in my head to Walk Off into Sunsets caliber.

Afterward, we flooded onto the street with the rest of the sweaty, punked-up crowd. A few people recognized me and pointed . . . but this was hipster-ville, so we managed to make it to our waiting car without people breaking their cooler-than-thou acts by coming up to us.

"If there were to be some major planetary event and the end of the world were to happen right now," Meg said happily, "I totally wouldn't care." She reached into the car refrigerator and pulled out a bottle of water. "That rocked."

I grabbed a water for myself. "So, don't get too unrocked, because Robin, from *Country Day,* wants us to meet her at Angel."

"Do you think there's a part on *Country Day* for me?" Meg asked. "Like, couldn't you have some diva tantrum about how you simply can't film another day without having me there to support and amuse you?"

"It would be *so damaging,*" I sniffled dramatically, "to my psyche." Then, just to be goofy, I changed my voice to be like a reporter's. "So, Annie, can you tell us what it's like to be New York's most infamous teen?" I stuck the water bottle into Meg's face like a microphone.

"Like, I totally, completely, don't know what the fuss is all about," she said in a fake Valley Girl accent. "Like, come on!"

"What about moving from Alabama to the city?"

"Like, who wouldn't? And compared to some of my Alabama antics, nothing I've done in the Big Apple is, like, any kind of a big deal."

"Can you tell us about your style sense? Who designed tonight's gown, for example?"

"Why, this ole thing?" Meg said, changing to a Scarlett O'Hara voice. "I just whipped it up out of some curtains."

Simultaneously the three of us collapsed into giggles.

Jason gazed at us warily. "You guys are weird. You definitely are."

———

Angel was, well, just about as heavenly and celestial a place as its name would suggest. When we drove up, I got that same excited, quivery feeling that I had the night of the *Country Day* party. There were some photographers lurking outside the door (I've learned to recognize them by now), so I grabbed Sarah's hand and flashed a grin.

"Why are they taking our picture?" Sarah whispered.

"Because you're with me and that's what they do."

Inside, everything was silver—walls, floor, columns. There were poofy white couches and these strange silver egg-shaped things that kind of looked like this ride at the West Alabama County Fair, except instead of seats there were *water beds* inside.

Robin shrieked when she saw us.

"Kittens," she howled, tossing one arm around my neck and one around Jason's and swiveling her hips in time to the techno beat.

Reflexively, I swung my hips with her. "This place is awesome."

She gave a small woohooing catcall. "Isn't it?" Then, she let go of me and reached out for Sarah and Meg and drew them into our circle. We bopped around for a while, until the DJ changed from techno to something horrifyingly atonal. I mean, I try not to be a music snob; it's not that I want to mosh to Stravinsky or anything, but I do kind of find melody a basic requirement.

"Wow," Sarah said, wiping sweat from her forehead. "This place is crazy."

"I know, awesome." I grinned. "I am so glad you guys came to visit."

"Yeah, it's great. I'm getting sort of tired, though. Do you think we could maybe head home soon?" Sarah asked.

I was not at all tired. I sort of felt like I'd been mainlining electricity—if that were possible—all night.

"Oh," I said aloud. I saw Robin, who had temporarily vanished, coming back across the floor with a waiter holding a tray of drinks. "I think Robin may have gotten us drinks," I said, only semi-apologetically. The subtext of this was: We can't possibly go home if there are drinks.

"Blue Sky," Robin said, handing me and Sarah each drinks. "You can't come to Angel and not have a Blue Sky." She passed drinks to Meg and Jason.

I swallowed about half my cocktail, ignoring Sarah's pleading look. I mean, did the girl come all the way to New York to go to sleep? Whatever. Not when Annie Hoffman was one of her best friends.

"We just need to get different music," I announced.

"You gonna tell them so, *princessa?*" Jason teased.

I drained my drink. "Why not?" Taking Jason's virtually untouched drink from his hand, I zigzagged through the silver egg beds to the DJ booth.

"Hey," I announced, poking my head through the door. "I was wondering what's going on with the music."

"So, Annie Hoffman has an aversion to the Driveling Pygmies?" Like everyone else in my new *Country Day* city-slicker world, the DJ was outrageously sexy.

"Annie Hoffman has an aversion to music without lyrics. Any chance we could get some eighties going?"

"Like some electroclash stuff?"

"Sure, that works" I answered, wondering what electroclash was.

The DJ ran a hand through his falsely platinum hair. "By the time you get back to the dance floor, you'll be a happy girl."

Somewhere along the trip, I had managed to finish Jason's Blue Sky. Suddenly I realized that I was a little—OK, definitely very distinctly—loopy. It was this weird, blurry combination of feeling totally energized but also like I might suddenly deflate if you were to stick a pin in me.

"Success," I announced, when I got back to the group. At that moment, Human League's "Don't You Want Me" started blaring through the club.

"Retro!" Robin screeched. "I love it. You're too much, Annie."

Clambering, I followed her on top of one of the white couches, not even thinking about the fact that the crocodile shoes might leave dusty streaks. I'm not an exhibitionist. Really. Usually, I prefer to shrink into a small, unavailable bundle rather than be publicly obvious. But there was something sort of fabulous about just being able to be unbelievably freaking crazy after all the trauma of the past couple weeks. I reached a hand down to Meg to drag her onto the white couch, but she shook her head and mouthed something at me.

"Can't hear you," I screamed to her, throwing my arms over my head and belting out the rest of the song. Angel, as far as I knew, didn't have a no amateur-karaoke policy. Madonna replaced Human League; then Bon Jovi replaced Madonna.

I loved dancing.

I loved dancing on top of a couch.

I loved being Annie Hoffman, instantly recognizable TV star.

I stretched a hand down to Jason and pulled him on top of the couch beside me. Wrapping my arms around his neck, I bounced against him happily.

"Having fun?" I asked.

"It's OK. I think Meg and Sarah really want to go home, though."

"They should get up and dance," I said. "Like, they never get to do this stuff at home."

"It's late, Annie. They're tired and I'm tired, too, to be honest."

He touched the top of my sweaty head. "Do you want me to take them back to your aunt's and come back for you?"

"No," I said grudgingly. "They're my guests—and my friends. I should get my stuff so we can go."

Springsteen came on, "Dancing in the Dark."

"But could we just wait until after this song?"

chapter 33

Is it possible that retainer wearing is a good indicator of personality? Because Sarah *always* wears hers, I generally try to and don't, and Meg hasn't even opened the jumbo package of Efferdent her dad got for her the day she got her braces off.

Flash forward to present-day shopping in SoHo: Meg got red pleather pants, I got black, and Sarah got none.

"I just can't, y'all," she said, pivoting in the black pants in front of the mirror. "I look like a bad Halloween costume. If you made masking-tape bones on my legs, I'd be a skeleton." She fingered the pleather dubiously. "This stuff is sort of disgusting anyway. Like I'm wearing congealed chemicals." She shuddered. "Gross."

"Sarah, come on," I said. "You look great."

"You really do," Meg threw in. Unlike me and Meg, Sarah is tall, and the pleather made the most of her extensive legs.

"We'd match," I noted.

"No," Sarah said. "Definitely not. I just can't fathom where I'd ever wear them."

"What's wrong with trig class?" Meg asked, snickering. "I'm definitely planning to flaunt these babies during third period."

"I dunno; biology might be more appropriate," I added. "You could showcase your concern for animal welfare by modeling fashionably faux materials."

"At the same time as I dissect a fetal pig?" Sarah began stripping the pants off. "Sorry, guys but you'd have better luck getting me to wear an actual Halloween costume to class."

"You're getting the cami, though, right?" I asked.

Sarah fingered the silky gold top. "Oh, OK. Twist my leg."

Back in our normal clothes, we circled through the boutique and piled our purchases on the checkout counter. The way my (astonishing) salary works is a bit strange; it's all put into some account to which I have zero access (an accountant manages it), but I have a credit card and a bank card and an allowance. My allowance usually seems really big to me, but I was definitely going over with Meg and Sarah's Excellent Adventure. Not that this was keeping me up at night or anything; it's my money, really.

I pulled out my credit card and laid it on the counter.

"Can I touch it?" Meg asked, making a big show of putting her finger on the card. "Oh, Annie, you're sooooo cool." She winked at the saleswoman. "You know she's a big star, don't you?"

The saleswoman smiled. "I know," she said.

"Well, then where's our red carpet? Our fluttering confetti? Our complimentary champagne?"

The saleswoman looked uncertain.

"Ignore her," I broke in. "She can't help being obnoxious. It's a fatal condition. One of these days, she's going to expire from an overdose of irritatingness."

"Irritatingness?" Meg asked. She sighed dramatically. "The stardom has gone to her head." She leaned over the counter and said, confidingly, "She was always a little, you know." Meg tapped her head knowingly. "*Daft.* But it's just been getting worse. They say that it's all over when language gets affected."

"I'm daft? Oh, right. Well, then we're going down together, sweetie."

"Hey, y'all," Sarah interrupted our banter. This was probably good, because Meg and I can kind of go on like that forever. "Look at this." She brought over a delicate gold bracelet, made to look like a vine with small roses twining through it. "Isn't it great?"

"Well, it doesn't go with pleather," I said, "but I love it."

"Hey, are there more?" Meg asked. "We should all get one."

"Not with roses, but there are other flowers," Sarah explained

The saleswoman, hearing our conversation, spread some of the bracelets onto the counter. In the end, Sarah got roses, I got daisies, and Meg got what I think were lilies.

"We match," I said with satisfaction. "Let's all wear them Monday morning and then I can think of you guys wearing yours."

"Uh, can I take it off for the fetal pig?" Sarah asked.

Twenty minutes later, we were curled up on fake toadstools in Jacques Torres with cups of cocoa made with dark, dark chocolate.

"Ummmm," Sarah said happily. "This stuff is amazing."

"Crane took me here," I said. "He lives almost just around the corner."

"Tell the truth," Sarah said. "Is he anywhere as luscious as he looks on TV?"

"Better," I said wryly. "Maybe I'll see if he wants to meet us after the show tonight."

"If we can make it an early night," Sarah said. "I'm still recovering from yesterday."

"Last night was fun," I said. "I don't get to see you guys that much anymore. It's worth celebrating."

"That wasn't about us," Meg said. "You barely talked to us. You were, like, off on top of the couch pretending to be Paris Hilton."

"I wasn't pretending anything," I retorted. "Why didn't you guys join me? You just stood there like barnacles."

"It was two A.M. We'd asked to leave like three times. You didn't tell us sleep deprivation was part of the New York package."

"I thought you'd have fun going out."

"Hey," Sarah broke in. "Y'all, stop. Last night was fun, especially the concert. I just thought we could maybe get home earlier tonight 'cause I'm sort of tired."

I sat there sullenly. Why was this whole conversation making me feel like Pluto getting thrown out of the solar system?

"Hey, aren't you Annie?" Two girls descended on our table. "OMG, I can't believe it's *you*," one squealed excitedly.

"We *love* the show," the other chirped.

"Great," I muttered. Normally, I really like talking to fans, but this was so not the time.

"Is it fun to work with Crane and Robin?" the first girl asked. She had a lot of acne and glasses and, frankly, did not look like the prototypical *Country Day* fan.

"It's fine," I said. Could they not see that I was in the middle of an intense personal experience that did not include *people I had just met*?

"You're our favorite character," she continued, pushing her glasses back up her nose. She was wearing a Lands' End jacket. I used to have one a lot like it.

"Thanks," I said, then added, "sorry, we're in the middle of something. Do you think you could leave us alone?"

Even behind the big glasses, I could see the girl's eyes cloud with hurt. Oops. Maybe I could complete my transformation into Cruella DeVil by ingesting live newborn puppies.

"Sorry," she said quietly. As they walked off, I saw her friend put an arm around her.

"Sorry," I echoed to Meg and Sarah. "I didn't mean it that way." They exchanged a look. I played with my napkin and pondered the unfortunate truth that I had just crushed some girl's fantasy of me. I wanted to teleport myself to the actual nonplanet of Pluto.

"Look, I agree with Meg," Sarah said at last. "Let's just make it an early night. We'll go to the show and then back to your aunt's for a sort of slumber party."

"Only if you brought unicorn stickers and sparkly nail polish," I said, still a little hurt.

"Anyway, I can't wait for the show tonight," Sarah—the eternal peacemaker—added. "You got the tickets, right?"

"Yup."

Sarah really, *really* wanted go to a Broadway play. Since we're both obsessed with musicals, I'd promised to arrange tickets for *Wicked*. Then, Hallie told me about this hot new musical that was opening that very night.

"I can't wait," Sarah said. "I've wanted to see *Wicked* for the longest time."

"Wellll," I said, happy to redeem myself, "I have a surprise even better than *Wicked*."

"What?" Sarah asked, taking a long sip of cocoa.

"We're going to the opening of this really hot new Broadway show instead. It's also a musical, but it's set in London. It's supposed to be very *My Fair Lady*–ish, only about punk rockers instead of flower girls."

Neither Sarah nor Meg looked particularly enthused.

"We're not going to see *Wicked*?" Sarah asked.

What was her problem? This was the *opening* of a brand-new show. I'd had to get the head publicist at Spider to pull every string known to mankind to get us three tickets, and there would be tons of celebrities there.

"It'll be the coolest thing ever to get to an opening of a show," I added. "Robin says this play's going to sweep the Tonys."

"Oh," said Sarah. "Sure."

"I wanted it to be a surprise," I added. Forget Pluto. Meg and Sarah were looking at me like I was from the Andromeda galaxy.

"Thanks," Sarah said dully.

"Jesus, Annie, what is *wrong* with you?" Meg exploded. "We've only been talking about going to see *Wicked* since you moved to New York. Don't you care? Or is it all about being a star at the hottest events for you now?"

"I thought it would be fun." I felt myself getting heated also. "It was a lot of trouble to get these tickets. Why would you want to see a show that's been around for, like, five years when you could be at the premiere of the musical that's about to be the biggest ticket on Broadway?"

"I'm sure they're both great," Sarah said placatingly. "Why don't you tell us about it?"

Meg muttered something.

"Let's just go," I said, very irritated. "I'm sure we can scalp the tickets and get into *Wicked* if it means that much to you." I threw my cocoa cup in the trash and headed out.

"Annie," Meg said apologetically. "Wait."

I just kept walking down the street. My cheeks were flaming. The next time Meg and Sarah came to New York, they could plan their own freaking trip.

chapter 34

In my next life, I want to be reincarnated in some kind of non-verbal culture. First of all, I would lose the capacity to humiliate myself every time I opened my mouth. *And,* as a bonus, I would never have to memorize lines again. It didn't matter that I was currently curled with my script on Jason's couch while he did a translation from Old Icelandic and absentmindedly played with my hair. The only way life would improve would be if I suddenly and spontaneously developed a photographic memory.

"Why is trash so much more fascinating in the abstract?" I asked aloud.

Jason mumbled something Nordic sounding. "Huh?"

I repeated myself. "I mean, this would all be very cozy if we were watching *Country Day*-ish bad TV or if I were reading a trashy novel. But I can't even get through the first two pages of this," I waved the script, "without getting so bored that I have to start compulsively picking my cuticle for entertainment."

"That's because it's work masquerading as play."

"I don't think I like working very much," I said grumpily. "Maybe I'll go petition the actors guild for fewer scenes each week."

"Great idea, Comrade Hoffman," Jason said sarcastically. "All those washed-up strugglers living in studios in the Bronx and working two waiter jobs just to be able to pay the ConEd bill are going to be really sympathetic to your plight."

I picked my cuticle a bit more intensively but said nothing.

"Why don't you go practice violin?" Jason asked.

"I don't feel like it," I said. "I don't like the piece I'm doing at the moment."

Jason reached out for the script and flipped through it. "If you wait a bit, I'll be done with my translation and can run lines with you."

"OK."

Rather than listen to Ancient Icelandic mutterings while risking a self-imposed, semi-deforming cuticle infection, I gave Jason a kiss and went to find his roommate, Pete.

"I decided to bother you," I announced as soon as I opened the door. Then I realized that Pete's girlfriend, Maria, and her roommate, Janna (whose name, appropriately enough, is pronounced "yawn-a"), were there, too. They were sprawled on Pete's futon watching none other than—ta da—me flirting with Jake/Jared on television.

"Eeewwww," I moaned. "Turn it off." For effect, I added, "You live with, what, like the smartest person on the planet and you watch this crap?"

"Well," Pete answered, "you're dating the smartest person on the planet and you star in this crap."

"Oh, that's so different," I said, watching myself walk, the camera panning my very tight jeans. It was probably a photography trick, but I looked sort of amazing in them, even better than in my thrift shop Levi's. The list of items to swipe from wardrobe grew even longer.

"Why?" Janna asked. "Don't you find it distressing that your appearance on this show is a tacit endorsement of characterological dysfunction?"

Excuse me? Was that even English? I know Jason says he likes his friends because they make him feel normal and not like some crazy prodigy. But honestly? They're kind of weird.

Since it had been about two weeks since I swallowed my last

thesaurus, I just shrugged in reply. There was an awkward pause.

"So," Maria said, breaking the silence, "I think you should introduce me to Crane Renfrew."

"What?" Pete gasped. "I make you pasta, homemade from Grandma Stefanucci's recipe, and you're going to ditch me for the guy with the dimple chin?"

"He's gay," I said automatically.

"Really?" Maria sat up. "I had no idea."

Awkwardly, I remembered Crane's confiding in me. "Well, I probably shouldn't have said anything. He's out, but not like out in the *Enquirer* sense."

"Celebrity hypocrisy," Janna commented.

"I hate this part," I added, practically cringing as Berry, pouting, flung herself into Crane's lap.

"So, wait, now you're hitting on *Jody*?" Maria asked.

"Just to make Jake jealous."

"This whole Berry-goes-wild thing is bugging me," Maria said.

Yeah, well, join the club.

"But I bet it's spiked the ratings," Pete said.

"Right," Maria said thoughtfully. "Collective social titillation."

Although I spend a considerable portion of time *feeling* like an idiot around Jason, hanging around Jason's friends makes me think I actually *am* an idiot. It was time to return to sanity.

Back in Jason's room, I asked, "Are you done yet?"

"Ummm, soon, I promise. Go call Meg or something."

Normally, calling Meg is an activity that could conceivably take hours. But things still felt sort of funny between us, even though we'd ended up having a great time for the rest of the weekend and they'd *loved* the punk musical. Instead, I called Robin.

"I'm bored," I announced.

"Well, darling, let's remedy that. How does Club Cleo sound? I'm heading down in a few."

Club Cleo, frankly, sounded fantastic. Except . . .

"I don't have my lines for tomorrow done," I admitted. (And even though Jason was obviously more interested in 700 B.C. than me at the moment, I shouldn't ditch him, *particularly* to go dancing. Jason doesn't like clubbing because he thinks it's superficial—which I guess is true. On the other hand, if I worried about every part of my life that was superficial, I would have to give up *Country Day* and move to a remote island off the coast of Fiji and weave palm fronds for entertainment.)

"Sweetie, I've seen your scenes," Robin coaxed. "You're kissing and not much else."

She had a point there. "OK, just for an hour," I gave in without much of a struggle.

After we hung up, I went into the bathroom and redid my makeup, lining my eyes with a smudger, the way Max had shown me. Then I knocked on Jason's door.

"Baby, I think I'm going to go home. I can't get much work done here." The lie slipped out easily. It was really for Jason's benefit, I justified, because he'd be upset if he knew I was going dancing.

"Really? I'll be done in an hour," he said automatically. "Hour and a half, tops."

"By then, I'll have to leave anyway. I have to be up tomorrow at six."

"Well, maybe I could take a break and help you with your lines now," he offered.

"It's OK. I'll do my lines on my own." I grabbed my script, guiltily kissed the top of his head, and headed downstairs.

When I wandered into Club Cleo, Robin was holding court with at least seven exquisite guys, one of whom was Karl Kasaki. Robin had claimed they were done ("as in *finito, bella*"). Famous last words, I guess. No pun intended.

"Hey." I sat down in a chair that one of the sexy guys pulled up for me. "I'm Annie," I announced to the table.

There were a few snickers. "We know," said one of the guys, handing me a drink.

I set the glass down without even taking a sip. "I so can't," I explained. "I have to go home and finish learning my lines for tomorrow. I am here just for the briefest moment of necessary distraction." Which meant it was high time to carpe the diem. "Anyone want to come dance?" I asked.

"Too early," Simon St. Onge said.

"I don't dance," Karl said.

"What?" I cried. "Oh, please." I grabbed his hand and led him onto the floor. Simon was right—there weren't many people there—but that was no reason not to get things started.

It wasn't until the third song that Karl started getting a little, well, extremely gross. I just wanted to dance, but his hands somehow were constantly on my lower back, or thighs, or pulling me closer. Even when I kind of backed away, he would grab me and start grinding around on my leg. I couldn't believe this was Karl Kasaki; he was acting more like Joey Galaskovich, this nasty feel copper back home with a serious sweat gland problem. When Karl's hand floated onto my butt for the third time, I just left it there. But when the song ended, I made a big show of how out of breath I was.

"Whew, I'll be back in a minute," I said, and immediately went to go hide in the bathroom.

Robin was already in there, talking on her cell phone in an extremely irritated voice.

"I *said*, I get it," she spat into the receiver.

I made a "should I leave?" signal, but she shook her head and made a gagging motion with her finger.

"I'll talk to you tomorrow. Bye." There was a pause. "*No.* Good-bye." She flicked the phone closed.

"Everything OK?"

"Fine." She shook her head. "I can't believe you were dancing with Karl. You must finally be ready to ditch Toga Boy."

"What do you mean? We were just dancing."

"Don't be so naïve. That was the most manipulative thing you could have done. You *know* that it'll be all over the papers that you danced with Karl." She leaned close to the mirror and studied her lavishly applied eyeliner.

"I didn't mean it like that," I said. "Are you *serious*? That's ridiculous. We're just having fun."

"Gotta learn to be more careful, then. Mark my words: You'll be news."

I felt sick. Jason was not like my parents. He read "Page Six" and celebrity blogs every day just in case I was mentioned. He was so going to know that I had lied to him, and I had no idea how I could possibly explain that it was only because I didn't want him to get upset.

"Why do they *twist* everything?" I spat angrily.

Robin applied a microscopic amount of gloss to her already shiny lips. "People mostly have sad, boring lives and this is a way to feel better about that."

That was kind of strange.

"Anyway, I need another drink," she finished, capping the lip gloss and returning it to her purse. "Let's go."

I paused. "I think maybe I should just go home."

"Your choice." She blew me an air kiss and vanished.

I pulled out my own cell phone and immediately dialed Crane. "It's Annie," I said as soon as he picked up. "I goofed up again. Like really goofed." Quickly I blurted out how I had lied to Jason and that Robin said it would be in the papers. "And now I'm trapped in the bathroom and I'm a total idiot and I'm afraid to leave because someone will take a picture of me." I was talking so quickly that I could barely understand myself.

"Hey," Crane said calmingly. "It's OK. I promise."

"No, it's not," I wailed. I would seriously join a Tibetan monastery and take a vow of silence for the rest of my freaking life if it meant I could avoid explaining this stupid, pointless night to Jason.

"Come on, calm down," Crane repeated. "Here's what's going to happen. I'm going to call a car for you. In ten minutes, go to the back of the club. It's on a creepy alleyway, but trust me, you'll be safe and there's not going to be many photographers on a weeknight anyway. Why don't you text Jason right now that you're going to my place to practice your lines? Which is the truth, because I'm getting out my script and making some tea and just waiting for you to get here." He paused. "This is not a reason to panic, OK?"

"OK," I answered feebly. "I'm on my way."

chapter 35

Forget being nonverbal. In my next life, I want to live in a world where there are no alarm clocks and every morning will begin with me gently entering the realm of consciousness filled with energy and vitality.

"Uhhhh," I moaned, reaching out a hand to slap my alarm off. Then I realized that I was lying on Crane's couch beside him. The sound hadn't been my alarm after all but Crane's phone. I blinked, trying to remember why I was in his apartment. The dregs of last night filtered back to me slowly.

"Oh *no!*" I bolted upright and shook him. "Crane, we fell asleep. I never went home!"

"What time is it?" Crane asked groggily.

"I don't know." What did it matter? "My aunt has got to be freaking out," I said unnecessarily as Crane's phone started ringing again.

"It's seven fifteen," Crane blurted. "I forgot to set an alarm. Shoot, shoot, shoot." He looked at the ringing phone. "This is the car service. I'm sure of it." He sat up. "Yeah, so sorry. I'll be there in a minute." He looked at me. "Come on, we've got to go," he said insistently. "We should already be on-set."

"I need to go home," I protested automatically. The sun hadn't even risen and my day was already approximating total disaster.

"No, we have to get to the set, Annie. We're totally late." He grabbed my hand. "Come on."

On the way to the set, I tried calling Aunt Alexandra about

twelve times to let her know that I was all right, but she didn't answer the phone.

"I guess she's still asleep," I told Crane. "I mean, she never gets up before eleven anyway, so I doubt she noticed I didn't come home. She's as bad with alarms as I am." I reached into the refrigerator for a pomegranate juice. "Thanks for talking me off the ledge last night," I added. "That was really nice of you and I'm sorry I made us late."

"Oh, don't worry about it," Crane said. He made a face. "I just kind of wish we would get there so I could actually brush my teeth."

"Yeah," I sighed.

When we finally ran into the makeup trailer, it was total chaos.

"Girl, you have had us setting off an all-city alarm," Max exploded.

"Annie, where have you been?" Gilbert asked more quietly. His voice was eerily calm. It was really unusual that he was here; Gilbert appears on-set with all the regularity of Halley's comet. I knew it was silly to be scared, but I took a step back anyway.

"I went over to Crane's." Gilbert was so obviously angry and this was so obviously awful that my words came out in a raspy half whisper. "To memorize lines. We fell asleep by accident."

"Your aunt was knocking on my door at one in the morning, panicked that you hadn't come home. She called Jason and he said you'd left hours earlier. We were about an hour away from calling the police. And your cell phone was turned off."

I closed my eyes, trying to ward off the sick, fearful feeling. If Aunt Alexandra had called Gilbert and Jason, she had obviously called my parents as well. I was in so much trouble that I might as well go lock myself in a padded cell for the next three decades of my life. "I didn't realize the phone was off. I'm sorry. I'll call my aunt."

Gilbert shook his head. "You need to get started on hair and makeup. These delays throw us totally over budget. Gretchen!" he called to a PA. "Call Annie's aunt and tell her she's fine."

Gretchen, who probably had been tucked in bed at 9:00 P.M. like any other adequately responsible human, chirped back agreement at Gilbert. I shot Crane a horrified look and headed off to get my hair washed.

I was only three-quarters orange when Gilbert reappeared beside me in makeup. I sat up a little straighter—trying to pretend I was the sort of eager-beaver actress who had shown up on time with all of her lines memorized and without triggering a police alert.

"It looks like you're not the only one in trouble today. Robin hasn't shown up yet. She's proving pretty unreliable, so we need to start restructuring some of the future scenes."

I nodded, relieved that someone besides me had taken over the title of Most Likely to Be an Inconsiderate Screwup. (Which, frankly, was completely fair, because if we were taking relative disasters, I was like a tornado that maybe ripped up a trailer park and Robin was more like Hurricane Katrina.)

"We had a meeting and we agree that it makes most sense to have your character fill in more. Robin was scheduled to film the car crash scene tonight. We're going to have you be in the crash instead."

"Really?" I asked aloud. Robin's car crash was part of a pretty intricate and major plotline. I hoped she wouldn't be irritated that I got the spotlight instead. "How?"

"So, this fight with Jake today will not end with you storming off and getting a ride home with Jody, but with you being stranded. You're going to sneak into Jake's car and drive it off."

I thought about it. "For revenge?"

"Well, the writers are reworking the script now, but I think the idea is more out of rage and desperation."

"What about the stuff we were supposed to do today?"

"We're going to start with Hallie's scenes with Frank and Katrina." He gestured to the makeup. "You can probably wash that off and just hang out. I'll let you know what the plan is for you, but given the situation, there's no point in filming any of your scenes until we know for sure where things are headed."

I tried to suppress a grin. I mean, that stank for Robin . . . but it's an ill wind and all that. Besides, now I had time for a nap.

chapter 36

If Aesop were to concoct a fable about my day, the moral would be that there are some days when achieving consciousness can only result in cataclysmic humiliation. Sure, the early bird may catch the worm—but the snoozing bird doesn't even care that there are worms waiting to be caught. (To say nothing of why anyone—even a bird—would want a worm when there was the possibility of a lightly foamed skim cappuccino?)

At any rate, I had been completely zonked out in my trailer for I don't know how long when Melinda from wardrobe banged on my door, then briskly entered.

"Gbhhbbrrrum," I mumbled as she tapped me awake. There was a grubby streak of orange makeup across the couch pillow. (Unfortunate. That stuff is impossible to get off; it has a wax base which makes it particularly adhesive. Short of clawing it off with my fingernails, I've yet to find the best option.)

"Change of plans," Melinda said briskly. "Robin's still not here, which means we need you in a cocktail dress today, not Monday. So hop up and let me see how much alteration we need to do."

Groggily, I sat up and reached for the fountain of blush-colored chiffon.

"Pink?" I asked. "I don't think I do pink."

Melinda said nothing but gave me a look that plainly stated, *There are children running naked through the streets of Kyrgyzstan and you dare to complain about couture?*

Well, yeah. When it's *pink*.

The pink dress made me look about five. Given that we were filming a scene where I basically act old and bitter, I'd have been happier in something sleek and black and that didn't totally swallow me to the point where I looked like an Oompa Loompa at Easter.

Jake/Jared, meanwhile, was taking our big fight scene very seriously. "You really think I care about that?" he snarled at me.

"No," I protested, a beat too late. Even though the setting and timing of scenes were different now, The Writers had managed to salvage a lot of the original dialogue. This was good news for people who had stayed home last night to memorize their lines—*moi* not included.

A blank look crossed Jared's eyes briefly, which probably meant I had missed some key line. "Give it up, rich girl," he continued. You can't buy your way out of this one."

Right. Now I remembered the line I was supposed to say before. "I don't think you care about anything," I backtracked. Then, for good measure, I threw in the line I actually should have said at this point: "I don't need to buy my way out of this because there's not a problem."

"Cut!" Dana the director announced just as Jared started to talk. She strode onto the set. "OK, Annie," she said quietly, so only I could hear. "What's going on? This is the third time you've wrecked your lines."

"Sorry," I apologized. "I'm just a little addled. You know, all these changes are really sudden."

"The script is virtually the same, Annie, with just a different setting."

"Sorry."

"Do we need to break so you can actually memorize your lines?"

"*No,* I've got them down. I promise."

Dana made a funny pursing motion with her lips. She's one of those people who can seem irritated at the sunniest of times. Now she looked like she was channeling Lucifer himself.

"Let's take it from the kiss, folks," she barked, heading back to the sidelines.

Obediently, Jared and I started tonguing.

"Are you messing with me?" he asked.

"No." I leaned forward. Was there something else I should have said there? I quickly glanced at Dana, but she didn't look any more displeased than she had a minute ago.

"Berry, I don't know. I think you're using me to get at Jody."

"Why would I want Jody?"

"You think I'm dumb, don't you? You think I'm your trashy little bit of boy toy."

There was a pause. "No," I squeaked, hoping that what I said was actually in the script and not just instinct.

"I know what you're up to. I know that you're collecting from Celia Lincoln and I know you're using that money to buy off Snider Green."

"So?" That was *not* what I was supposed to say, but I couldn't remember anything else. Maybe I had an actual memorizing disability, rather than just chronic memorizing boredom.

Jared looked sort of blank. "So, you think I care about that?" he asked. Then he shook his head. "Cut," he said. Then, he announced "Sorry, I can't do this."

Dana flew in between us. "What's going on?"

"I can't do it if she doesn't get her lines." He looked really angry.

"Come on." Dana put an arm on his shoulder, but he shook it off.

"I'm serious!" He said it loudly enough to be almost a yell. "Covering for her like this is insane. It's making my performance look bad and it's keeping me from getting into character and . . ."

I stopped listening as he went through his actor lingo. Jared takes himself *very* seriously. Apparently, his last show involved people wearing full-body gray makeup and crawling across the stage while quoting Proust. As he pronounces it, he is an act-*or*.

"Dana. I'm telling you, I'm fed up with it," he complained at the top of his well-trained lungs. "Every day it's the same thing. I realize it's a high school drama, but do we have to maintain a high school level of professionalism?"

"OK," she said soothingly. "Come on." I stood there awk-wardly as she led him off the set, where they stood talking for what seemed like forever. Jared was gesturing wildly and Dana appeared to be saying reassuring things that had absolutely no effect.

"OK, everyone, take a break," she called loudly after a while. "Half an hour, OK. Get some coffee or whatever."

As I started offstage, she shook her head. "Stick around for a second, Annie, OK?"

Grand. I was getting sent to the *Country Day* equivalent of the principal's office while being forcefully ensconced in the world's largest and pinkest tutu.

chapter 37

If bad things happen in threes, embarrassing things evidently happen in thirteens. In the wake of the Jared-needs-anger-management disaster, we'd rescheduled most of our afternoon scenes and filmed stuff that either didn't involve a lot of dialogue or used people other than me and Jared. During a break, I called Jason but just got his voice mail. I really hoped he wasn't avoiding me. At this point in my jaded career, I knew it was too much to hope that the pics of me and Karl hadn't leaked—but with any luck, Jason had had a crazy morning and not gotten a chance to check the celebrity gossip sites bookmarked on his laptop.

Most everyone except for me and Dana and some of the crew got to leave by six. We had to hang around so that I could film the reworked car crash scenes, which had to be done after sunset. So I went back to my trailer and inhaled the salad that someone had gotten for me. Given that I was working a seventeen-hour day, you would think they could have managed something like, say, Chinese. Something substantial, so I wouldn't be tempted to gnaw the hem of the gargantuan pink dress, which I was still wearing and which was cutting into my armpits the way I imagined an iron lung would.

My cell phone rang when I was devouring the last shred of carrot. I hoped it was Jason, but one glance at the caller ID sent me into spasms of despair.

"Oh, Helena, I'm so sorry. I completely forgot," I said, skipping the hello.

"You were supposed to be here an hour and a half ago," she announced. "This is the second lesson in a row you've missed."

"I know; I'm still on-set. I haven't had a moment to breathe and I completely forgot to cancel the lesson. I'm so sorry." Situations like this probably called for energetic gushing, but I was too exhausted to manage anything more than a semi-whimpered apology. Anyway, maybe it was good I'd missed the lesson. . . . I hadn't exactly had a chance to practice the way Helena liked this week—or month—to be honest.

"I'm really sorry," I added again. "I'll see you Thursday and I won't be late; I promise." *And,* I thought to myself, *maybe by Thursday I'll have had a chance to practice and maybe I won't have spent the preceding twelve hours constantly apologizing for my entire existence while wearing a thoroughly appalling couture tutu.*

Pretty much right after I got off the phone with Helena, there was a knock on my door.

"Come in," I said, tugging on the sharp boning of the dress in annoyance.

It was Gilbert. I hadn't realized he was still here.

"How are you feeling?" he asked.

"OK." I rubbed my eyes, well aware that the worst day known to mankind wasn't going to end anytime soon.

"These scenes are going to take a couple of hours to film; I know you've been here all day, but we've got the location all arranged, so I hope you can soldier through."

"OK," I said again. It wasn't like I thought I'd be lucky enough to get sent home with a world-famous foot masseuse or anything.

"I thought we could ride over to the location together."

I shrugged. "Sure." I tossed the dregs of my salad and grabbed the bag with the mangy clothes I'd worn to the set that morning.

When we were settled in the car, he asked, "So, how are things going?"

"Oh, fine," I lied. Luckily it was dark, so he probably couldn't see the instantaneous scowl that appeared on my face.

"I know there's been a lot of tension on the set and it seems like you're in the thick of it." Gilbert sounded almost apologetic.

"I know. I already talked to Dana. I thought I'd gotten my lines down, but I guess I overestimated. I'm sorry it caused problems." *With the world's most pretentious act*-or.

"It's not the first time, Annie." We were quiet for a moment.

"I know," I said again. Maybe some toxic chemical had been released in the atmosphere which was infiltrating people's brains and making them say the same thing *over and over.* I goofed. I get it. Can we please move on?

"You're also chronically late to set. It costs a lot of money each time we have to delay filming, and we can't afford another Robin situation."

I sighed. This was incredibly unfair, because *everyone* except for His High Pomposity, King Jared of Explosiveworld, was chronically late to set. I'd even had to wait for Max on occasion. I mean, if they would stop asking us to come at *dawn*, things might be different. And, OK, I know Robin's dad is a big deal. But why does she get to break the rules without anyone saying anything to her? Ever?

"I'm not the only one," I defended myself.

"No, but it's got to stop, kiddo."

"OK," I parroted. Given that we were trapped in the backseat of a car, this whole experience was giving new meaning to the phrase "captive audience."

"It's just that [blah blah blah]."

I tuned out as Gilbert droned through his explanation of why my being late was responsible for intense budgetary crises that depleted Spider's net worth, which caused the NASDAQ to drop, which meant the national deficit quadrupled, which meant less aid to needy developing nations, which meant unstable global functioning, which meant the end of the world as we know it. Yes, all because I overslept. When he paused for air, I said emphatically, "I get it. It's not going to happen anymore."

Gilbert smiled and gave my shoulder a sort of awkward half pat. "This isn't easy work, is it? I hope it's not too much for you. You've gotten raked through the tabloids in a way we never anticipated."

"It's OK." I stared down at the expanse of pink fluff. Maybe if I clicked my heels together three times, I would suddenly be transported home. That would be ideal. Instead, my cell phone started ringing. It was my mother. Fabulous.

"Annie, where were you last night?" she demanded

"Nowhere."

"Well, I've just talked to Alexandra and she's very distressed and, frankly, so am I. You're a sixteen-year-old girl in a strange city. You cannot stay out all night."

I didn't think I'd been lectured by so many different people in a single day before. I was so not offering myself up for another recap on why I was the most horrific person on the planet.

"Mom, believe it or not, I'm still filming. I'll call you later."

"Annie, no," she said loudly. I hung up anyway.

Gilbert glanced over at me. I turned away from his glance and stared out the window for the rest of the trip.

By some miracle of long-overdue karma, it only took a few minutes to film me running, distraught, through a parking lot. Then we got a couple close-ups of me unlocking a car door. There wasn't any dialogue, but Dana had me put on a sort of nasty-looking sneer.

"Nice job, Annie," she said. "I think that's a keeper."

Visions of takeout danced through my head. I could almost see myself flopping down on my bed, chopsticks in hand.

"Now we just want to get a couple of you driving away, sort of crazily, through the parking lot."

A very strange and sickly feeling came over me. No one had said anything about driving.

"Driving?" I asked.

"Right. Gunther's installed a camera in the car. We want you to drive down to the end of this row. Look furious and upset. That same sneer would be great. At the end, you'll jerk the wheel hard."

"I actually have to drive? I can't just sit and sneer in the parked car?"

Dana said something, but I couldn't really hear her because there was this strange buzzing sound in my ears. I looked around for Gilbert but didn't see him.

"I thought there was going to be a stuntman," I added.

"For the actual crash, yes. He'll be here in a bit. We usually use the actors for this part." She looked at me. "They said you could drive; wasn't that right?"

The buzzing in my ears intensified. I would never, ever have agreed to these scene changes if I'd known the car crash involved my hands actually touching a steering wheel.

"I don't like it," I whispered.

"What?" Dana said. "I can't hear you."

I shook my head because I doubted that I could open my mouth without throwing up. This had all the makings of another classic Annie Hoffman Hurlocentric Automotive Experience.

"Let's get going, then." Dana turned and walked back to the side of the camera. I wanted to call after her, to tell her I couldn't—unquestioningly, absolutely *could not*—do this, except no sound was coming out of my mouth, just a weird choking sort of panting sound. I was going to be sick. Really, really sick. The sort of sick that couldn't be caught on film because it would be censored by whatever Standards of Human Nausea Board existed.

I shut my eyes. *It's just driving. You've done it before. It's just in a parking lot. Just get it over with; then you can go home.* Slowly, I opened the door and sat down. This was all Robin's fault. I mean, what was wrong with that girl? If she were even a marginally responsible person, *I* wouldn't be saddled with this nightmare.

Grimly, I turned the key in the ignition, and the car roared to life. What twisted nutcase had invented the concept of a fake car crash anyway? Talk about bad juju.

In five minutes, it'll be done. Aware of the camera beside me, I did my best to sneer.

And attempted to breathe.

Tentatively, I pushed down on the gas pedal. The car began the familiar lurch forward. Like Dana wanted, I accelerated. I was suddenly—disgustingly—sweaty. If my heart beat any faster, it would probably self-combust from friction. Tears streaked down my neck and into the crevices of the awful dress.

I couldn't do it.

I just couldn't.

Slowly, I braked and got out of the car. With the spotlights trained directly on me, I made my shivering, sweating, nauseated way off-set. Dana and Gilbert ran over.

"I'm not doing it," I choked. "I can't."

"Annie," Gilbert said.

"I'm just not. Sorry." There was snot running down my face. My dress was sticky with sweat and tears. I was undoubtedly the most revolting person ever to wear a ten-thousand-dollar tutu.

"Hey," Dana said. "I'm not sure what's going on, but—"

I cut her off. "I don't want to hear what you have to say," I screamed.

At that, even the people who were pretending not to stare turned to look at me. Embarrassed, I grabbed my bag and ran as quickly as my jellyish legs would allow.

"Hey, girl," Jeremiah said, as I dove into the backseat of the car.

"Just take me home."

He looked at me and then, obviously, at Dana and Gilbert and everyone else.

"Get me home," I repeated.

chapter 38

It used to be that I would wake up the first morning of summer vacation with the most delicious feeling—like there were just days and days of bliss stretching ahead of me. The morning after The Most Atrocious Day of My Entire Life, I woke up with the reverse of the summer-vacation feeling—just awful, like maybe I'd somehow ingested an aardvark and the few remaining days of my pitiful life would be consumed by surgical removal of the snout that pierced my stomach. I stared at the ceiling and contemplated secretly immigrating to the Cayman Islands to sell scuba equipment.

Finally, at around eleven, I managed to get out of bed. If I hadn't been officially fired for running off-set last night, I undoubtedly was now that I hadn't even shown up. Sighing, I picked up my cell phone. Thirteen new messages. I turned the phone off, found a trashy mystery, and crawled back into bed.

I was almost done with my second mystery when there was a knock on the door. I ignored it; so far, denial seemed to be working pretty well as a life strategy.

"Annie?" The voice was too deep to be Aunt Alexandra's. I rolled over. It was Jason.

"I'm hibernating," I muttered.

"Give it up." Jason picked his way across the room, still scattered with yesterday's clothes, and sat down on my bed. Were I not so overwhelmed by general wretchedness, I might have been embarrassed by the state of the room. Jason had never been in my bedroom before, but I'd been in his. The guy has a five-second rule for clothing; he's too obsessive to allow a single garment sully the floor for more than a moment.

"I'm not mad," he said. "Really. I just want to know why you lied to me about going home the other night."

I shut my eyes for a moment. I'd almost forgotten that little bit of idiocy. "You saw me on the Web," I said softly. Of course. It was absolutely inconceivable that a single action in my life might somehow not be publicly broadcast as an act of Satan. "I thought you'd be annoyed that I was going out and I didn't want to have to justify myself." There was a pause. "It was dumb," I said. "I guess you heard about yesterday also."

Jason nodded.

"Do you think I'm going to be, uh," I stopped, "fired?"

Jason snorted.

"It said in my contract a bunch of stuff about failure to show up and not having memorized lines could result in termination," I added.

"They're not getting rid of you," Jason said confidently. "They're more worried about Robin's nonstop absences and, besides, Berry's the hottest character on the show right now."

"Well, are they very mad?"

Jason shrugged. Even such a slight movement made his bangs fall into his eyes. I realized that my own hair was still crusted with gel and volumizer and the other products from filming yesterday. I wondered if he'd seen the gossip columns about me. Probably. How else would he know that I was in dire need of rescuing and that it was time to clatter up on a white horse of cheerful, yet blasé, optimism?

"Come on, you think you're the first person ever to storm off a set? Especially after working, like, what, fifteen hours?"

"Fourteen."

"Exactly. They would *never* make Robin or Hallie do that.

They know they wouldn't put up with it." He leaned forward and planted a soft kiss on my drool-caked cheek.

I wasn't buying it. "Please go," I muttered, turning back to the wall. "I like my cocoon of misery."

"Give it up," he answered, tugging me upward. "Go take a shower. We're going out."

"I can never show my face in public again."

"The sooner, the better. The story's already leaked."

I turned back to him. "What do you mean?"

Jason took my hand and pulled me back down to sit on the bed beside him. "OK, don't freak, but it's on the Internet, which means it's going to get picked up by the mags soon."

"What's the story?" I asked, horrified.

"Annie Hoffman, teenage diva, storms off set and messes up filming."

"But . . . ," I protested.

"Don't worry; they'd say that even if it weren't true."

"It makes it sound like I left for no reason." I rubbed my eyes blearily and mascara came off on my fingers. I'd been too upset yesterday to care about Max's nighttime face regimen. "No one told me I'd have to *drive*." I stopped, not sure how to explain what happened.

"Annie, it doesn't matter," Jason said. "Forget it. Really. Let's go do something fun."

I looked at him doubtfully. Then it dawned on me that I pretty much had nothing left to lose because I had, well, lost it all.

Can I just say that the entire world can crash down around your ears, like the dusty end of an apocalyptic horror movie, and it doesn't matter as long as you are in the greatest city on earth? Jason and I ended up cabbing down to the East Village, where he talked me into trying on all these totally wild vintage clothes. I sort of felt like I was a little kid playing dress-up in most of them—tropical seventies prints aren't generally my thing—but couldn't help cracking up with each new garment he tossed into the dressing room. Afterward, we took a really long walk and ended up on the Lower East Side. I had never been down there before. I had no idea there were so many restaurants and bars. Or *piercing* shops.

Suddenly I knew what I wanted to do. This was *my* freaking life. I mean, if I was going to be touted as a total diva bad girl, shouldn't I at least get something I wanted out of the deal?

"I want to get my eyebrow pierced," I said calmly.

"Seriously?" Jason asked reflexively.

I nodded. "Absolutely. I've wanted a pierced eyebrow for a very long time, and if I'm going to be called a brat I might as well act like one." I grinned. "Let's go."

Jason gave me a wary look. "Are you sure Berry can have a pierced eyebrow?"

"I have some news for you and the rest of the entire world. I am not Berry Calvin." I grabbed his hand and marched us into the shop. "Do you do eyebrows?" I asked the clerk behind the counter. This was probably unnecessary. In addition to a spiky, dyed-black fauxhawk, the guy had his own eyebrow pierced. Also his nose, lip, and ears (four times right ear, twice left ear).

He nodded languidly. "Which one?"

"The right. Definitely." I perched on the stool and tried to ignore the suddenly crawly feeling I had. This couldn't hurt that bad. I mean, thousands upon thousands of people have survived eyebrow piercings. As risk taking goes, it's hardly like, I don't know, bungee jumping or skydiving or whatever. And the fauxhawk guy was carefully scrubbing his hands, up to the elbows, then putting on plastic gloves, just like a surgeon would. He reached over to a white, cubelike thing and pulled out a plastic package, which he popped open to reveal a surprisingly long, silver hook.

"What is that?" I asked suspiciously.

"Gotta use a piercing needle for the brow." He looked up. "Don't worry; I just grabbed it from the sterilizer."

Had I been capable of screaming, I probably would have. Unfortunately, my standard terror response is neither fight nor flight but a more depressingly catatonic freezing. (I have no idea how my prehistoric ancestors survived. It seems like woolly mammoths would have devoured the few Neanderthals dopey enough to stand completely still and wait for the onslaught.) So before I unfroze enough even to whimper, the guy grasped my head, tilted my face back, and pinched the small nub of flesh above my brow bone. Gently he cleaned the skin with alcohol and made a small mark.

"Does this look like the right place?"

Mutely I nodded. He grasped the skin more firmly and poked the needle through. It went through surprisingly fast, sort of like a rough pinch. My mouth unfroze itself.

"Mmmph," I grunted in surprise.

"All done," said the fauxhawk. "Which one of these do you want?" He held out a small case with different rings. I pointed to a smallish, plain silver one. In another second, he had tipped my head back and inserted it. He held a mirror in front of me.

"Wow," I said happily. "That wasn't bad at all." Slowly, I closed my eye and scrutinized my brow. I had wanted this piercing for so long and, well, honestly? It was just as cool as I'd thought it would be. Three cheers to me for abandoning my doormat status long enough to get what I wanted.

It was about time.

chapter 39

The next day was Thursday. I really would have made a special effort to show up for filming all bright eyed and bushy tailed, except that Gilbert left me a message giving me the rest of the week off. This was, as far as I was concerned, inescapable proof that having a temper tantrum was completely advantageous. Forget silver linings; this was more like the glittery splash of a full-on Swarovski-encrusted gown.

At any rate, there didn't seem to be much of a point hanging out at home when the entire Big Apple was waiting for me to take a chunk out of it. So I ended up at a sushi restaurant in TriBeCa with Robin and a tableful of frankly exquisite guys, all of whom professed great interest in my distressing week.

"So, what, you're storming off-set now?" Karl Kasaki gave me a languid wink. "Talk about a temper, baby."

"No!" I squealed. "They always make it sound so bad. That's not really the way it was at all." I popped a piece of yellowtail roll in my mouth. I have decided that I love, love, love sushi. I thought it would be slimy, but it's not at all.

"So, how did it happen?" Simon asked. Simon has a really strong accent, which meant that what he said sounded more like "'ow did eet 'appen?"

"It was already a bad day and I just really don't like driving and when they said 'car crash' I didn't realize I was going to have to drive and I just freaked and left." I rolled my eyes at Robin, before I realized that she wasn't looking at me because she was devoting every morsel of energy to flirting with this guy named Nick, who wasn't having anything to eat or drink because he was training for the Olympics in beach volleyball. I realize it probably takes a superhuman amount of muscular effort to qualify for the Olympics in anything, but I have to say that beach volleyball is not exactly the decathlon.

"Wait," Karl said. He refilled my cup with sake. "*You* were supposed to crash the car."

"No," I giggled. "They had a stunt double for that. I was just supposed to drive it a few feet through a parking lot."

"And you freaked?" Simon asked.

"I don't like driving," I repeated.

"Sounds like a tantrum," Karl teased.

"*No,*" I squealed again. "I just got upset." A shrill ring cut through the conversation. I reached for my phone and glanced at the caller ID. It was Jason.

"Hey, baby," I drawled happily into the phone. "What's going on?" I crooned, heading into a hallway outside the restrooms. I hate talking on the phone in front of people. I mean, it's kind of hard for people *not* to listen when you're spewing in front of them.

"Where are you? Is everything OK?"

"Yeah, why?" I fingered my brow piercing absently.

"I thought you were coming over here."

I was? "Oh, I didn't realize we had, like, final plans. Sorry," I apologized.

"Where are you anyway?"

"Getting sushi. With Robin and Karl and . . ." I started listing off people, then realized I didn't actually *know* all these people's names, which was kind of unfortunate, given that I'd just blathered intimate details of my personal life to them.

"I made lasagna," Jason said bluntly.

OK, I don't even like lasagna. Jason should have remembered that.

"Sorry," I repeated again. This was hardly the most enlightening conversation on the planet. Karl and Simon may not have had Jason's brainpower, but they definitely had to have gotten a refill on sake right around now. "See you tomorrow instead?"

"Tomorrow?"

"Well, what should I do? You can't really want me to drop everything and head up to Columbia now? I'm having fun." Besides, I was a wee bit tipsy.

"Well, don't let me interfere with your fun," Jason said icily.

"Stop it. I didn't mean it like that." Had he always been this sensitive?

"You could have fooled me." There was a click.

He hung up on me. My own boyfriend had freaking *hung up* the phone on me. My life suddenly seemed like a bad *Saved by the Bell* episode. Or maybe I was trapped in some sci-fi movie where my actual life morphed into my drama-centric *Country Day* life.

"Yeah, well, good-bye to you, too, buddy!" I snapped into the already-beeping receiver. "Creep," I added loudly for good measure.

"Annie, hey, was that Jason?" a voice behind me asked.

Karl. The guy seriously needed to leave me alone for five seconds. "Yeah," I turned around to face him, "but he's—"

The words flew out of my mouth and hovered there, midair, as I realized that the voice *hadn't* belonged to Karl but to some photographer who had followed me. Did these people have a celebrity GPS system implanted in their cameras? As I stared at him in horror, he clicked away three, four, five times. My eyes began to water from the flash.

"Come on, already," I snapped. There was another click. "Maybe tomorrow I'll invade *your* private dinner and *your* private phone calls by taking a bunch of pictures of *you*," I added, with all the scathing dignity I could manage.

chapter 40

If you were to go inside the brain of someone brilliant and rational, like Stephen Hawking or Albert Einstein or, frankly, even Jason, it would no doubt be clean and orderly, with neural circuits looking as shiny and functional and unidirectional as actual pieces of freshly stripped wire. If you were to go inside my brain, I'm sure it would be as rusty and grime covered as the engine of a Ford Pinto that'd been sitting in a junkyard for twenty years. Chronic confusion and addlement will do that to a mind. Seriously, it wouldn't surprise me if someone came out with a study that bubble tea eroded mental clarity. Because I had been drinking bubble tea every day for about the past two months and I swear I had never been as totally, irrevocably, wildly confused as I was now.

Jason and I managed to patch things up the next day with all the requisite mushiness, and we had a totally nice night on Friday just hanging out in his apartment. Here's what I didn't get: How could it be that sometimes Jason and I had so much fun and sometimes things felt all weird and touchy? It was like we had the Jekyll and Hyde of teen relationships.

All of this was kind of on my mind when I headed out for a walk in Central Park the next afternoon. Normally, I wouldn't make a special fashion effort just for a walk. But, given my rising profile, I spent time concocting the perfect casual teen-idol-in-autumn outfit: skinny jeans tucked into supershiny black boots, a leather jacket swiped from wardrobe, and a newsboy cap. I think the entire outfit was probably worth more than Jules makes in an entire year. Once I figure how to get men with excessively gelled hair and expensive camera equipment to stop stalking me, I will tackle the cosmic injustice of the American labor system.

On the way back to Aunt Alexandra's, I stopped off on Columbus Avenue to go shopping again. It was all in the interest of maintaining my image, which I hope negated the fact that I managed to spend triple my monthly allowance in about an hour. I was back at home preening in front of the mirror when Jason showed up.

"Smashing," he said

"Really?" I asked happily.

"Oh, *dahling,* absolutely."

I paused. "You're playing with me."

Jason smiled. "Maybe a little."

"I'm trying to improve my image."

"By wearing a shirt the size of my fingernail?"

I shrugged. "More like by just thinking about what I look like and what I do, because I seem to be getting stalked a lot."

"Yeah, do that. Because you being a megabrat reflects on me."

I stopped. Jason *sounded* like he was kidding, but maybe Mr. Hyde was baring his fangs again.

"Do people say things about me to you?" I asked bluntly.

"Well, yeah, of course they do. But don't worry about it. Really."

I hate being told not to worry. It's like being told not to have skin. Like as if I could control it, I would. "Well, what do they say?" I asked Jason.

"It's stupid. Don't worry about it. I shouldn't have brought it up."

"*What* do they say?" I repeated, suddenly angry.

"Just updates, you know. 'Page Six' says you were late to set and didn't know your lines or whatever." He touched my hair.

"It's stupid, Annie. I don't take it seriously and you shouldn't either."

"Your friends read 'Page Six'?" I asked.

"As a cultural experiment."

Riiight.

"I used to *like* being famous," I pouted.

Jason rolled his eyes. "You still do."

"No," I said disagreeably.

"Oh, come on." He poked me in my side.

"No."

"Maybe just a little?" He tickled me and I wriggled away.

"No." There was a pause. "So where should we go tonight? Robin says there's going to be this amazing party downtown."

"I thought we were going to the Film Forum with Maria and Pete and people."

Vaguely, a memory of talking to Jason on the phone this morning floated through my head. At that point, I'd been sort of out of it and awfully tired and would have probably agreed to donate my firstborn to an experimental colony where only Latin was spoken.

"They're showing *The Philadelphia Story*," Jason continued.

I felt my nose wrinkle. Pete and Maria are nice and everything, but they're not incredibly interesting . . . and Maria would probably bring along Yawna and Yawna might bring along her other, even more awful friends. Like, Maria is nice and Yawna can be tolerable, but Yawna's friends are the sort of people who think that brainpower increases in direct proportion to length of armpit hair.

"Well, I just got fun new clothes," I said persuasively. "I think I should go flaunt them."

"You flaunted last night," Jason said. "And Thursday night and all last weekend. I thought you loved old movies."

"I just don't feel like it tonight. I've had a hard week."

"It's not like I'm asking you to do manual labor. I just want us to hang out with my friends for a change."

I made a face.

"I thought you liked Pete and Maria," Jason cried. Normally, I hate for Jason to get upset, but today I really didn't care, for some reason.

"Well, yeah, they're nice and everything," I said. "But they're *so* serious and Janna always comes and suddenly we're talking about structural covariance or something."

"That happened once."

"I just want to have fun tonight," I pouted.

"And, what, you can only have fun when somebody is buying you an endless stream of twenty-dollar blue martinis? Sorry, but I just don't get the same thrill you do from sauntering past the bridge and tunnel crowd into a private entrance."

"I just happen to prefer dancing to engaging in pointlessly pretentious dialogue."

"Yeah, it's so much better to party with a bunch of vapid, name-dropping cyborgs. I hate the way you act around them. You totally change, Annie."

"I do not."

"You do," he insisted. "You get all giggly and stupid. It's like watching Sybil go through a personality change."

Excuse me?

"Not one of those people is even remotely human," he continued.

"They're my friends," I fought back weakly.

"Only because you're on *Country Day*. You think they'd give you the time of day if you weren't sneaking thousand-dollar boots out of wardrobe?"

"Shut up," I said. "They like me. And the fact is, I *am* on television."

"For how long if you keep acting like this? Listen, *princessa,* how many tantrums and days of not memorizing lines do you think Spider will put up with?"

A cold chill came over me. That was definitely not what Jason had said the other day. "They expect me to be a diva," I retorted.

"Right. Look, do whatever you want. You seem to have lots of practice in not thinking of anyone besides yourself."

"That is so not true!" I realized I was screaming.

"Annie, I'm sorry, I keep trying to give you chances, but frankly, you're not the girl I feel like dating right now. I don't want to keep scraping your drunk self off the floor after you've spent all night flirting with other people. Go whoop it up with guys who appreciate that garbage."

"Yeah, and you go enjoy decomposing in Deadville," I spat out. Jason turned and walked out without another word. I realized I was shaking.

How had that happened?

chapter 41

Forget Jason. For-get him. There were sexy guys galore in this world. And they all *did* like me.

"Would you like me even if I weren't on *Country Day?*" I murmured to Simon St. Onge. We had left the party we originally went to and somehow ended up at another one way downtown, in the back room of a club. It was a small place and sort of dingy, even though it was supposed to be some exclusive soiree.

He refilled my flute with champagne. "Naturellement," he purred in my ear.

"Really, really, really?"

He nibbled my earlobe in reply. I giggled. His tongue tickled.

"I love champagne," I announced. "Except it makes me tired." I put my head down on the table.

"No." Simon lifted my head up. "We must dance."

I allowed myself to be led from our booth toward the overcrowded dance floor. It was so packed that it was difficult to walk. I eventually fell onto an oversized ottoman.

"No sleeping, baby," Simon said, as he plopped down beside me.

"No," I mumbled, leaning back. I was beginning to have a bad case of the spins. I put a foot down on the floor to steady myself.

"Simon?" I asked. "How much champagne did I have?"

"Not sure, *bébé*. Why?" His hands were smoothing my hair, caressing my cheek, moving down my body, resting in the curve on the side of my stomach.

"So beautiful, *chère*," he whispered.

"I'm dizzy," I said. Vaguely, I became aware that he was kissing me. I closed my eyes and let myself be petted. There were other guys instead of Jason. Really. Guys who *enjoyed* sauntering through private parties. Guys who matched my own level of glamour and cool.

I'm not sure how long we'd been snuggling when Robin crashed on top of us.

"I said, I like it here, can I stay?" she sang off-key.

Karl piled on top of Robin. "What are you lovers doing?" he demanded.

"I have the spins," I said. "Too much champagne."

"Too much?" Karl asked. "Or not enough." Somehow, another ice bucket had appeared on the table beside us. Karl leaned toward it and grabbed the chilled bottle. Without bothering for a flute, he took a healthy slug and passed the bottle to Robin.

"OK, I want some," I said. My words were slightly slurred: "I wannnsome." Somehow, when Robin passed the bottle, we tipped the ottoman and the four of us crashed to the floor, shrieking and giggling. The champagne fizzed everywhere, drenching us and the floor and other people nearby.

"My head," Robin moaned, crawling between us to stand up.

"Forget your head," Karl snickered. "My champagne."

"May I help you?" One of the party promoters stood above us. I stuck my hand in the air and he pulled me up. A busboy appeared beside us with a stack of towels.

"These things should be more stable," Simon said, grabbing a towel and dabbing his shirt.

The promoter made apologetic murmurs.

"Can we get you anything else?" he asked.

"Yeah," I answered. "More champagne." Robin, Karl, and Simon dissolved into loud laughter. Encouraged, I added, "And a personal injury lawyer. Ms. Field has damaged her head."

"It was already damaged," Simon said. His hands circled my waist.

The guy looked at us uncertainly and then moved on.

"What now?" Robin asked.

"Did you dance on the bar here?" I asked her drowsily.

"No. That was made up."

"Pity," Simon said.

I stared at the bar. "Let's do it."

"What?" Karl said. "You have the spins."

"All the more reason."

Laughing, we made our way over to the bar, which was dark wood and very tall. Even with me in my spikiest heels, it came all the way up to my chest. The wood looked old.

"Yes?" asked the bartender, gliding smoothly over.

"Outta her way," Karl said. He and Simon boosted Robin onto the bar. She let out a joyous whoop and threw her arms over her head. Simon held out his hand and I stepped onto it, and in a second I was up there myself, spins and all, for the whole room (forget that, the whole *world*) to see and envy. Teetering, I let out a whoop myself. To make everything that much more fabulous, one of my favorite Karl Kasaki songs came on just then. Robin and I squealed and bopped and blew air kisses to Karl. Around the room, I saw people pulling out their cell phones and snapping photos of us.

Forget Jason. I was born to this kind of fame.

We'd been on top of the bar for quite a few songs when I became aware of a tapping on my ankle. I looked down and a man with a mustache and dark blazer was motioning to me. I bent down.

"What?" I said. I had to scream because the music was so loud.

He said something that sounded like "mumblemumblemumble." I stood back up and kept dancing. The man thwacked down on my foot hard.

"Ouch!" I knelt down. "What the hell!" I screamed.

"Miss Hoffman, I suggest you come down from the bar." I looked and saw Robin being helped down. Once on the floor, she turned and shrugged at me.

"We're just having fun."

"Please come down," the man repeated calmly. He held out his hand. "It's hard for people to get drinks while you're there."

"Just fun," I repeated.

"Miss Hoffman, if you do not come down, I'm going to call security."

For some reason, this struck me as extremely funny. Annie Hoffman, security risk. I started laughing.

"Phhwaa, security," I giggled.

"Miss Hoffman," said the man, "I'm going to have to ask you to leave."

"What?" I said.

"You're drunk and we don't want the poor publicity that's going to come with this sort of behavior."

"Excuse me," I said, then hiccuped loudly. I started over. "Excuse me, but I am not asking you to be responsible for my behavior." I glared at him and sat down, swinging my feet over the bar. "I am perfectly responsible for me all by meself." That sounded wrong. "Myself."

"Miss Hoffman, there is a long time between now and your twenty-first birthday. You're making it hard for us to turn a blind eye. You're welcome back here any night when you are not in this state."

"Are you kicking me out?" I gasped.

"I suggest you leave quietly, before this gets more embarrassing for you."

"You asshole." The words were out before I realized it. I had never called anyone an asshole before, but it felt surprisingly natural given the circumstances.

"Look, either you leave on your own or we have security escort you out."

I pondered my options and slid off the bar.

chapter 42

When I told Robin and Simon and Karl I was leaving, they laughed.

"Baby, stay!" Karl cried.

"Yeah, you can't leave," Robin chimed in. "I thought you said we'd be partying till dawn."

I snatched up my purse. "I don't appear to have a choice." I gestured to the waiting manager. "Asshole," I added, mortified.

"They're kicking you *out*?" Robin gasped. "Oh, they have another thing coming."

"I'll go talk to them," Karl said. Then he belched loudly. This was the guy whose softly tender ballad lyrics had defined my middle school existence?

"Don't bother," I said disgustedly. I waited for someone to offer to come with me. Silence.

"Why don't we all go to Club Cleo?" I said. "Where they, you know, appreciate us."

Robin looked at Karl. Karl looked at Simon. No one made a move to go.

"Fine," I said. Storming away, I burst through the front door and smack into the blinding glare of a thousand flashbulbs.

"Oh my God," I said, feeling slightly ill. Instinctively I threw up an arm to shield myself, then realized I looked like a moron. There was a roar of people calling my name. How on earth did they get here *so quickly*?

"Annie, is it true you got kicked out?"

Flash click flash flash.

"Annie, any comment on whether your heels damaged the famous antique bar?"

Click click flash.

"Annie, is it true you cursed at the manager?"

Flash.

"Annie, we heard you didn't even pay your tab."

Click.

"Where's your boyfriend, Annie? Where's Jason?"

Flash click flash flash.

"Are you and Karl now an item?"

Click click flash flash click.

Dizzy with booze and flashbulbs, I tried to steady myself.

"Shut up," I muttered to myself. Then, louder, "Shut up." The words were out before I realized it. "*Shut up!*" I screamed at the crowd. "Just stop it," I yelled. "You maniacal, nasty creeps. You have nothing better to do than prey on people. You're like parasites." There were even more flashes exploding around me as I screamed, but I kept on screaming and screaming, the words tumbling over themselves in a stream of obscenities.

"Leave me alone!" I roared at last, so dizzy and angry that I could barely see. Tears were streaking down my face.

"Honey." A big man's arm circled my shoulders. "Honey, let's go." I could tell he was a bouncer. He led me into the middle of the stunned throng.

"Let us pass," he barked at the reporters. When they stood there, shocked and still clicking, he repeated himself: "*Let us through!*"

"You parted the paparazzi sea," I said automatically.

"Let's go," he kept repeating. "You're getting out of here."

A photographer leaped directly in front of us and snapped.

"Get the hell away," I screamed, and the guy did.

I started giggling.

"I don't know my own strength," I said.

The bouncer patted my shoulder absentmindedly and led me over to where a cab was waiting. He helped me into the backseat. The spins, which had been in remission, started up again. I could feel myself shivering dizzily.

"Oh, God," I moaned. "What just happened?" Tears, I realized, were still sliding down my face. "What did I just do?"

chapter 43

Aside from not being magically able to zap away pimples, the second worst thing about not being a teen witch was the inability to turn back time. Seriously. If only I could turn some silly device or wave a wand or hop into the Marty McFlymobile and redo everything. But because I had the bad luck to be stuck in reality, I had to go to work with what was either still a hangover or the most powerful sense of dread I'd ever had. I could practically feel it, like some toxic gray sludge, oozing its way from my toes up through my body.

The thing to do, I had decided, was just to be dignified and calm and pretend nothing had happened, sort of like Maria when she came back to the captain after running away and he's very coy and nosy about why she left.

(Except retreating to a convent rather than flinging yourself ecstatically into your crush's waiting arms does not exactly fit into the *Annie Hoffman Manual of Preferred Coping Mechanisms*.)

With a tremendous sigh, I opened the door to makeup.

"Well," Max preened. "Look who's been good enough to drop by."

"Hi," I said. Maybe if I stuck to monosyllabic words, I would manage not to humiliate myself any further.

"Now you promise you won't cuss me out?" he said.

"You heard about that?" I asked.

Max raised his eyebrows. I threw myself down in the chair. "Of course you did," I answered my own question.

"Now what is this?" He reached a finger down to my eyebrow

ring. I'd almost forgotten that I hadn't been back to the set since *last* week's disaster. "It's a bit nineties retro." Max paused. "Maybe we'd better take it out for filming."

"You can't take it out. It has to stay in for a month; otherwise the hole closes up."

Max looked at me for a minute, then tugged the ring out.

"*Max,*" I cried, clapping a hand to my stinging brow.

"I think you'll thank me later." He pointed to a television in the corner, where one of the morning shows was on. "You need to lay low."

I wandered over to the screen for a closer look, still massaging my eyebrow.

"And Senator John J. Devereaux of Louisiana says he is committed to improving teenage morality in America. After learning of Annie Hoffman's drunken Saturday night exploits, Devereaux said, 'It is unacceptable for our children to idolize someone whose behavior is so out of control. Ms. Hoffman obviously has serious emotional problems, and rather than glorifying her and putting her on TV and magazine covers, we should try to help her find her way in life. I am praying for that sad, lost little girl.' Senator Devereaux's opponent, former governor Joshua Browning, claims this is a shameless ploy for publicity and that Devereaux is simply trying to deflect attention from his own scandals."

The television cut to a shot of someone I assumed was former governor Browning: "I guess my opponent has realized the unfortunate truth that TV stars are more famous than us mere politicians. I say the senator needs to stop hitching his wagon to Annie Hoffman's star and get back to the real issues."

"Hoffman, the sixteen-year-old star of the hit show *Country Day,* verbally assaulted photographers after she was thrown out of a New York nightclub on Saturday for being drunk and disorderly." There was a quick video of me, looking wild-eyed and bleary and like I might pull a Mike Tyson and bite off some-one's ear.

I felt breathless. Was it possible to suffocate on your own mortification? Like literally choke on the lack of oxygen and die? Besides, I couldn't seriously be a political issue. I mean, I couldn't even *vote* yet.

"And Hurricane Lorraine is expected to touch down tonight off the coast of Florida. . . ."

I snapped the television off and stared, wide-eyed, at Hallie and Max and Frank, normal people who had managed to get through the weekend without catapulting themselves into scandal.

"What am I going to do?" I asked softly. "This is so unfair."

Hallie came over comfortingly and drew me back to the makeup chair.

"Just try and go about everything as normal," she said. "There are a thousand stories out there like this. It'll die down."

I looked at her uncertainly.

"It seems like a much bigger deal than it is," Hallie continued.

Robin, returning from getting her hair washed, joined us. "Paris Hilton went to jail," she said, adjusting the towel on her head.

"Winona shoplifted," Hallie said.

Max sighed. "*Britney,*" he said significantly.

"The point," Hallie continued, "is that they survived and you will, too."

"It's so embarrassing," I moaned.

"Well, sloppy," Max said, "maybe you should think about that before you curse out thirty photographers with video cam-eras."

I made a face.

"Think of it as charity," he said. "The sale of those videos is single-handedly putting a lot of paparazzi children through col-lege."

Midway through the morning, I was waiting to film a scene when I got a message from a very eager PA.

"Hi, Annie," she chirped. "Gilbert wants to see you." She smiled broadly. I wondered if she was going to go back to her NYU dorm and tell everyone that she'd been selected to bring Annie Hoffman in for tarring and feathering.

"Sure," I said aloud, sliding my feet back into my shoes, deep red stilettos that were probably causing permanent metatarsal damage, which meant that I would be both fired *and* crippled by the end of the day. Glumly I tailed the PA away from the set and back into the trailer area. Gilbert couldn't actually have an actual torture squad ready and waiting; that would only trigger more bad publicity.

Willing my tear ducts not to start their customary leaking, I followed the PA into the executive trailer.

"Anything else?" she asked perkily.

Gilbert shook his head. She left and I stared at the floor.

"I don't suppose I need to tell you that Saturday night should not have happened," he began. "When this story first broke, I thought there was some kind of mistake. I figured it was Robin or maybe even Hallie."

Why was everybody compelled to think of me as a goody-goody? I mean, if I'd had Robin's brat grrl reputation, no one would have even blinked an eye.

"So I'm going to tell you this: We can control this story once. I've got some people working on it. But if you keep this up, I can't fix it."

"I don't expect you to fix it," I said. The pattern of tiles on the floor was really quite interesting.

Gilbert thwacked a copy of the *Post* onto the table in front of us. "Read that," he said, pointing.

Looks like Little Miss Hoffman keeps getting too big for her Size 0 Rock & Republic britches. The teen star—previously known for hooking up with her tutor, inability to memorize lines, and chronic whininess—stunned paparazzi this weekend by unleashing a string of threatening four-letter words as she stumbled out of a private party at a hot TriBeCa nightclub. Sources tell us that Annie was asked to leave by management after refusing to climb down from the bar, where she was dancing and screaming.

I cringed.

"Annie, you need to figure out how to present yourself in public and figure it out fast." Gilbert looked like he had a lot more to say, but his cell started ringing. He glanced at the caller ID and shook his head. "I gotta take this. Yeah, this is Grayle," he said into the phone. "You're kidding me," he said, after a pause. "OK, I'm on it." He flicked the phone shut.

"Well, maybe I misspoke," he told me. "I thought we could control this, but it looks like you're on the cover of *People* this week. Target headline is 'Good Girls Gone Wild.'"

Really, there was nothing to say to that. I studied my cuticles. Probably the best solution was to embark on a "cleansing journey" that would take me to Tibet until I made enough money and connections to hire an evil scientist to give the entire American public collective amnesia.

chapter 44

I'd turned off my cell phone while I was on-set, which meant that I had nineteen new messages by the time I crawled into the backseat of the car to go home.

"Hi," I said to Jeremiah, reaching into the refrigerator for a POM Blueberry. I needed antioxidants to be able to face my voice mail. But I had barely twisted the cap off when my phone started ringing. I checked the caller ID. My parents. There were about a thousand things on the planet I would rather do than answer the phone, including testing electric cattle prods for potential short circuits.

"Hi," I said unhappily.

"Listen to me," Dad's voice boomed. "I don't want to hear any of that garbage about how the media exaggerate everything."

"Hi," I said.

He cut me off. "Or about how no one does anything worse than they do back at home. Or how hurt you are that we don't trust you."

"Dad," I said.

"Because I don't believe you."

"There's photographic evidence, Annie," Mom joined in. "I watched talk shows today; *The View* said you'd gone from being It Girl to It Drunk."

I burst into tears.

"Stop it," I screamed.

"You deserve to know what they're saying about you. You think you can live in fantasyland?"

"Leave me alone," I spat back. "They're handling it on this end. I already talked to Gilbert."

"*They're* handling it? You're our daughter," Mom cried. "And, you're coming back home. This is obviously not working out. You don't have the maturity."

"You don't know what it's like. I'm upset about this, too."

"I should hope so," Dad said. "The entire world says you're a troubled, bratty, manipulative drunk. Do you have any idea what it's like to hear this stuff about you?"

"We're making a plane reservation for you to come home," Mom added.

"*No,*" I yelled. Jeremiah turned around and raised his eyebrows at me. I shut the privacy panel, even though I was screaming so loudly that it probably wouldn't do any good. "You can't do that," I babbled. "The show needs me. *I* need to do this. Having me home won't change anything."

"So now you're permanently a nasty drunk?" Mom asked. "Wonderful. You're coming home."

"Please," I blubbered. I had a contract that meant I had to work at *Country Day* for a certain amount of time except in certain cases; I just didn't remember what those were.

"We're talking to the *Country Day* people tomorrow."

"They want me to stay." I wasn't sure if this was exactly true, but Gilbert had had about twenty chances to get rid of me by now and hadn't.

"What they want—or what you want—doesn't matter anymore."

"Look, I goofed up," I started.

"No, goofing up is when you set the house on fire cooking chapatis. What you did was not only illegal; it was unconscionably stupid," Dad said.

"Fine, I was stupid and irresponsible and I get that. And I am *mortified.*" Tears were streaking down my face and into the collar of my jacket. "But let me fix it. Please."

"We're calling the set tomorrow," Dad said.

"And no going out this week," Mom added. "You're grounded."

That was so absurdly unenforceable, I almost laughed at the same time I was choking over my tears. There was no way I could return to Tuscaloosa and being uncool and bad clothes and bad eyebrows and curfews and no boyfriend. "I have to keep doing this," I begged.

"Annie, it's not good for you."

"It is," I insisted. Then, because I really couldn't take any more, I decided to hang up. "Bye."

"What?" I could hear squawks on the other end of the line as I disconnected. I didn't care. I curled up sideways, buried my face in the sticky leather seat, and sobbed.

I don't know how long I spent like that, just huddled and crying, but when I finally stopped blubbering I realized that the car had stopped as well. I sat up. We were outside Aunt Alexandra's apartment building. I rubbed a hand across my eyes and opened the privacy panel.

"Sorry," I said to Jeremiah. "Have you been here long?"

"Doesn't matter," he answered. "You OK?"

No.

"Yeah," I said aloud.

"That politician, Annie," Jeremiah began, then shook his head. "I mean, maybe I shouldn't get involved. But that politician is using you and people know that. Don't worry about it."

"Yeah," I repeated, feeling like crying all over again. "Thanks."

I went upstairs. It was Aunt Alexandra's canasta night, so I rummaged through the take-out drawer until I found the menu for the Vietnamese place I like and ordered enough food to feed most of the Upper West Side. Then I turned on the television and flopped on my bed to wait.

"And whatever happened to Annie Hoffman? That's the question on people's minds after the teen star's exploits."

"Oh, *shut up*!" I snapped, switching off the television. Then, feeling silly, I turned the television back on and put in the *My Fair Lady* DVD. When the doorbell rang, I grabbed my wallet. It turned out not to be the deliveryman but Crane, holding an absolutely enormous bouquet of yellow roses.

"Rough week?" he asked, bending down and giving me a hug. I clung to him for a moment. I couldn't remember ever being so happy to see anyone.

"I'm such an idiot," I wailed. But before I could dive any further into my quickly becoming permanent pit of self-loathing, the guy from the Vietnamese place stepped off the elevator.

"You order delivery?" he asked.

I took the bill and rifled through my wallet. "Do you take cards?"

"Not unless it's over twenty dollars."

I looked at Crane, who smirked. "Five minutes here and I'm already buying you dinner?" he asked.

"I'm a manipulative brat, remember?" I said as we headed inside.

"But you're not." Crane unpacked the summer rolls. "You are giving me half of this food, right?"

"Yeah." I pulled down plates from the cupboards. "I think you're in the minority on the brat opinion," I added, launching a summer roll into the plum sauce.

"What you need," Crane said, "is a plan to reinitiate yourself as America's good girl."

"Sure, but what?"

"Let me think," Crane said thoughtfully, nibbling on a shrimp.

"You need to get the media to like you again. Preferably sometime soon."

For once, someone besides me stated the obvious. I reached across the table for another summer roll. "How did my perfect life turn so perfectly awful?" I moaned, but I was beginning to feel more optimistic. I mean, Crane didn't despise me even though I'd been a moron. Maybe the rest of the world could simply follow his exemplary lead.

Crane and I ended up spending so long over dinner we might as well have had a full seven-course meal instead of takeout. Somehow, we managed to come up with a reasonably viable Annie Hoffman Social Salvation Plan. After he left, I ran up the three flights of stairs to Gilbert's apartment and banged on the door. The instant Gilbert answered, I regretted it. He was wearing a nice suit and I could hear music and people talking in the background.

"Oh," I said. "This is obviously a bad time. I just wanted to talk to you."

Gilbert stepped into the hallway and shut the door behind him. "What's up?"

"OK, I'm really sorry," I said quickly. "I've been a disaster lately and I've messed everything up. I am so seriously sorry and if I could change everything I would. But," my voice cracked, "I think I have an idea about how to fix this, except I'm going to need you to help me." I was talking so fast that the words were tumbling all over each other. Quickly I sketched out the plan.

"Why should I help?" Gilbert asked.

Good question.

"Because I'm trying and because I actually want to be the great person everyone thought I was." I realized as I said it that this was the truth.

Gilbert looked at me thoughtfully. "I have to get back to my guests."

We had *so* not finished our conversation. "What about my parents?" I asked. "They say I have to quit the show and come home."

He winked at me. "Why don't you tell them just what you told me?"

"Well, what about everything *else*?" I called after him. If my life were a musical, Gilbert would be the Henry Higgins character who works major transformative miracles. I mean, how could he leave me dangling?

chapter 45

The next few days were nothing short of torture. If I weren't me, I might possibly have found Letterman's Top Ten Reasons Annie Hoffman Loves the Paparazzi mildly amusing. As it was, I found myself slinking past news kiosks, all of which seemed packed with magazines of my luridly drunk self. Pretty much every day after filming, I turned off my cell phone and crawled into bed. The next scandalous headline would probably be that Annie Hoffman had turned into the creature from the unwashed pajama lagoon. This transformation was not evident to everyone, I guess, because one day, as I was leaving the set, Robin asked if I was up for partying at Angel that night. I pretty much fell over. It was sort of like she'd walked into some bleak postapocalyptic land- scape and failed to comment on all the smoke and cockroaches.

At any rate, despite his less than ringing endorsement the other night, Gilbert put in a few calls and we managed to get my Social Salvation Plan under way. On Friday morning, Jere- miah took me to the airport, where a woman named Susan met me. Even in the private air terminal, the kiosks were stuffed with pictures of me flaunting my lurching self. Sighing, I stopped and pulled down a copy of *Us*.

"I, uh, just want to see what they're saying," I told Susan. Flipping to "Annie Hoffman's Wild Ride," I took in references to the "soused star" and that a whole lot of people seemed to think that I represented either the "tragedy of American youth" or "the degenerate next generation." In 72-point turquoise font, the headline screamed: "Can She Recover?"

I winced. "How much to buy *all* of these?" I asked the clerk, gesturing to the dozens of magazines splattered with my unfortunate image.

The clerk laughed uncertainly. I guess he thought I was joking.

"Never mind," I said. "I believe in freedom of press and that would be censorship." Regrettably.

"Annie?" Susan broke in. She had a slight southern accent that kind of reminded me of home. "We should get going."

"OK."

"Are you nervous?" she asked, as we walked across the tarmac.

I thought about that for a second. I mean, yeah, stars should be into this whole private-jet thing. Personally, though, I have to say that I would rather fly with a bunch of other people than get on the large housefly that Susan kept referring to as an airplane.

"Maybe a little," I said, gesturing to the tiny plane. "I mean, that pilot knows what he's doing, right?"

Susan laughed a tinkling laugh. "I meant about the rest of the day, not about flying."

"Oh," I said. Then I grinned. "I'm actually OK. I'm kind of looking forward to it."

The pilot apparently was competent enough, because we arrived in Louisiana with time to spare. Governor Browning himself was waiting for us on the tarmac.

"This is a gutsy thing you're doing," he said, shaking my hand.

I shrugged. "It was nice of you to stick up for me and, besides, I'll do just about anything to help this story die."

The rest of the day was insane. I thought I had been photographed a lot in the past few months, but it was absolutely nothing compared to campaigning with Governor Browning. We pretty much went all over the state, talking to hurricane victims near New Orleans and at a Town Hall meeting in the capital and ending up at this huge rally that night. The whole thing was pretty humbling. When I'd been off shopping and getting drunk and generally being a moron, there had been real people in Louisiana dealing with real issues. They were worried about unemployment and getting their homes rebuilt and I was worried that someone would know I'd worn jeans that were supposed to stay in wardrobe out clubbing.

"Annie, why did you decide to support Governor Browning?" a reporter asked as we walked past a cheering crowd on the way into the rally.

I paused and took the mike from him. "Governor Browning has a lot to offer the people of Louisiana. He *didn't* want to use me and my mistakes as a way of getting his name into the papers. I don't think there's a single person in this country who doesn't know that I've made some bad decisions in the past few weeks. I think what's surprising is not that this happened but that it got so much attention. At the same time as I'm trying to learn from all my mistakes, someone is putting those same mistakes on national television and calling it news."

I probably could have gone on like that for a while but opted to cut myself off before I turned into a dripping, sugary mess. "I hope you all vote for Governor Browning. Truthfully, the things that he and other politicians do are a lot more important than what people like me do." I handed the mike back, waved to the crowd, and headed into the rally with the governor.

It was 1:00 A.M. when the plane finally landed back in New York. Susan had arranged for a car to take me home. When I got to the apartment, I was surprised to see Aunt Alexandra still awake.

"Hi," I greeted her, kicking off my shoes. "Did I make the news?"

"More than, darling." I followed her into the living room, where she fluttered into her favorite chaise. I flopped on the floor in front of her. "Gilbert showed me how to record it." She clicked on the television and a picture floated onto the screen.

"Teen star Annie Hoffman made headlines today when she campaigned with Senate candidate and former governor Joshua Browning in the hotly contested Louisiana race." The announcer offered a brief recap of events as the screen played the by-now-familiar-but-still-horrifying video of me screaming wildly at the photographers.

"Darling," Aunt Alexandra said, "the next time you decide to make headlines, might I suggest waterproof eye makeup?"

I rolled my eyes. Because that had been *so* intentional. "I'll brush my hair, too, while I'm at it." Then I sat up a little straighter as pictures of today rolled past. There was a clip of me talking to a little kid in a homeless shelter and then the camera cut to my speech outside the rally.

"You look good," Aunt Alexandra said.

"I hope so," I said. "Do you think it'll make a difference?"

"Listen to this part." Aunt Alexandra turned the volume up.

"So, Jim, what are the repercussions of this?" a commentator asked.

"This is a very smart move by Joshua Browning; we are already seeing a surge in poll numbers. But it's also a smart move by Annie Hoffman. By confronting this problem head-on, she's not giving people a chance to keep criticizing her behind her back. It'll take awhile for Annie's recent exploits to die down, but I think people are now going to be talking more about this trip than about last weekend."

As the commentators switched to talking about polling numbers, I looked at Aunt Alexandra and grinned.

"Dare I say 'phew'?" I asked.

chapter 46

In terms of regenerative abilities, I was right up there with the starfish. I did a few more interviews, which Spider's publicists circulated to the moon and back, and a couple weeks passed, which meant some other unlucky star landed on the covers of the magazines. Because I wasn't going out much, things were kind of boring. When I looked for my violin, I realized it had been so long since I practiced that the case was kicked all the way underneath my bed.

On Tuesday, after I got home from filming, I walked down to Lincoln Center. Tuesdays were my regular lesson day, but Helena's door was closed. Slowly, I knocked. There was no answer. I could hear strains of distinctly un-Helena squawkiness filtering out from under the door. I knocked again.

"It's Annie," I called.

The door swung open. There was a small boy, about Nathan's age, standing with his violin in front of a music stand. Helena, towering over him, made her way outside and shut the door.

"Hi," I said awkwardly. I hadn't come for a lesson in kind of a while, but I couldn't help feeling just a tiny bit peeved anyway. I mean, this was *my* lesson time. How could she have given it away? "I guess I've, uh, been replaced?" I said questioningly, tilting my head toward her office.

"I left you a message almost three weeks ago saying that I was going to give away the time slot unless you started coming," Helena said bluntly.

Three weeks ago would have been during my not-listening-to-voice-mail-in-case-someone-said-something-I-didn't-like phase.

Aloud, I responded, "Sorry. I think that was during my not-listening-to-voice-mail-in-case-someone-said-something-I-didn't-like phase."

Helena's face moved slightly, like maybe she wanted to laugh. Encouraged, I added, "Well, I don't necessarily expect you to want me back as a student, but if you, um." I paused, then started again. "If you happen to have any time, I think I've finally gotten the Dvořák piece down."

Helena looked at me skeptically, so I added more sincerely, "I could probably use some help with the timing for the adagio section, though. I'm not sure I've slowed the tempo enough."

"What about everything else? The show, the partying, the other commitments?"

"I'm enjoying a pretty steady diet of crow these days," I said. "I have plenty of time for violin."

This time Helena did laugh. "My weekday schedule is pretty booked. If you're serious, I could do Saturday mornings at eight A.M."

Was she kidding? Helena knows I like my Saturday morning audible output to be limited to an accidental snore. I sighed.

"That sounds perfect."

After I left Helena's, I caught a taxi and went up to Jason's apartment. I purposely hadn't called first, because I was kind of scared he maybe wouldn't want to see me. So when he opened the door, I just stood there and let him stare, a bit hostilely, at me. I hadn't seen him since we'd had our big fight. He hadn't even called after I ended up all over the news.

"Are you going to say *anything*?" I said at last.

He blinked. "Do you think there's something we should be talking about?"

Uh, *yeah.* Was it possible that the smartest person on the planet had sold his brain on eBay?

"No. Course not." I made a face. "I dunno, Jason, aren't you at all upset about everything?"

"Why should I be?"

"You know."

"Why don't you tell me?"

I was beginning to feel like I was having a conversation with a Magic 8-Ball.

"I was really upset after that fight," I said softly. "*Really* upset."

"Obviously," Jason said.

"I've been a jerk for a while and that's not fair to you."

Jason raised one eyebrow. It's one of his sexiest expressions, which was not a good thing to notice since he was basically telling me to head back to Loserville without passing go or collecting two hundred dollars. On the other hand, I was getting really good at admitting blame. Probably this was somehow making me a better person in the long run, but it was getting tiresome. I'd rather just be reincarnated as a locust or something. "I don't know why I've been such a brat lately." I sighed. "I miss having fun with you."

"Been awhile," Jason said.

"Yeah." I was suddenly really, really tired of being Apologetic Annie. "Feel like going out?"

"Out? Where?"

I shrugged. "Wherever you want."

"Why?"

"Like a date, maybe?" My voice was so small I sounded like a laryngitic chipmunk.

"And I should go on a date with you because . . . ?" Jason asked, but he sounded like he might be teasing and not angry.

"Because I miss you and I'm hoping you miss me. And." I took a deep breath. "And because if I hadn't been such a horror show lately, I could call and get us Knicks tickets, except I don't think I should pull in any more favors."

"We could pretend like we're normal people and buy scalped tickets."

I thought about it. For once, being normal sounded pretty great.

"I'll get the tickets if you get the popcorn."

chapter 47

Even when you are a very famously bratty diva, there are still people in this world who are happy to serve and protect. For example, the Spider travel agents were falling all over themselves to make me happy. It sort of made me regret that I had such a boring request; I could probably have *literally* asked for the moon and they would simply have answered, "Oh yes, Miss Hoffman, the space shuttle is waiting at the launchpad." At any rate, as soon as I got off the phone with them, I called Meg. She answered on the first ring.

"So there is a plane leaving from Birmingham on Friday night, arriving LaGuardia at eight twenty-two P.M."

"Yeah?"

"So I thought maybe you and Sarah could be on it." I could almost hear the wheels churning in her brain. "Oh, come on," I said after a bit of silence. "It's taking you this long to come up with a snarky comment? Given current events in my life?"

"You *have* been a bit visible."

"But the good news is, I think I might have snapped out of it."

"Really."

"Oh, sure," I said blithely.

"Because I was thinking that the best way to solve your little issue would be to go into rehab. I mean, everyone's doing it."

"What I really needed was a voodoo doctor for an exorcism."

"Yeah. Sorry, Annie. I take full responsibility for this whole episode. I forgot to tell you. I've been sticking needles into a little Annie Hoffman doll."

I couldn't necessarily blame her. "Hypodermic needles filled with straight vodka, right?" I said aloud.

"Of course." There was a pause. Then Meg asked, "So I guess I'm coming to the Big Apple for the weekend?"

"I'll pick you up at the airport, even." I paused. There was no point in being a celebrity if I didn't flaunt it a *little*. "In a limo," I added.

"Can we go get your eyebrow pierced this weekend? Finally?"

Had it been that long since I'd talked to Meg? "Well," I began happily. "We *really* need to catch up."

I spent the rest of the afternoon shooting scenes where I console Hallie after Robin has wrecked her reputation. Given that this was about the seventieth time Hallie/Kit's reputation had been decimated, it wasn't the most novel plotline. (To say nothing of completely unrealistic; it takes far, far less effort and manipulation to destroy a reputation. You can trust me on this.)

"OK, everyone, that's a wrap," Dana announced at last. "Nice work today."

I glanced at my watch. Unbelievably, two hours had passed. "Bye," I called, giving a quick wave and heading to my trailer to change into jeans and a sweatshirt. On my way outside, I passed Robin. She and I hadn't really talked much in the past few weeks. Impulsively, I called after her, "Rob?"

She turned around.

"Jason and I are going out to dinner tonight. Wanna come?" I offered.

Robin pursed her enormous and well-lacquered lips. "There's a party I wanted to hit."

Ah, yes. I'd almost forgotten. The more things change . . .

Aloud, I answered, "Well, if you change your mind and you want to come out with us beforehand, you've got my cell."

Since we'd run over filming this afternoon, Jeremiah and I rather predictably got stuck in traffic almost immediately. I picked up the *Post* and flipped through it. There was absolutely no mention of me anywhere. I smiled despite myself. No news is indeed good news. Absently I turned to the horoscopes. Mars, it seemed, was ascending.

"Hey, Jeremiah?" I asked. "We're going to be stuck here for a while, right?"

"Afraid so."

"Do you think we could get off the expressway and go find someplace sort of deserted? Like a parking lot or something?"

"Why?"

"Well, do you think you could give me a driving lesson?" The words came out smoothly, without even a quaver. I sounded positively confident about this whole (potentially ludicrous) endeavor. "I'd like to get my license at some point." That sort of was the truth.

"Don't see why not," Jeremiah answered. "We're not getting back anytime soon anyway."

He signaled with his blinker to exit and we found a relatively deserted neighborhood street. Getting out of the backseat, I found myself surprisingly unqueasy.

"I'm not very good at this," I warned Jeremiah, as he slid over to the passenger seat.

"That's OK," he answered

I nodded, more to reassure myself than anything else. Planting my hands on the wheel, appropriately at 10:00 and 2:00, I stared at the empty road ahead of me.

What can I say? I'd spent a lot of time not knowing what to do, but it was finally time to accelerate.

acknowledgments

I am indebted to many people for their patience and support throughout this writing process, most especially my agent, Jenny Bent, and editors, Hilary Rubin and Becki Heller. My friends and family offered endless encouragement and advice; I'd particularly like to thank Jill and Lloyd Lewis, Michael and Camille Mendle, Chris and Nicky Mendle, Ann Frosch, the real Robin Field for (among other things) lending her name to a truly flawed character, Nicole Bond, Lisa Halliday, Anna Poppe, Jeanine Stefanucci, Paige Harden, Tara Peris, and Erika Meitner.